CONTEMPORARY AMERICAN FICTION

CITY OF GLASS

Paul Auster is the author of *Moon Palace, In the Country of Last Things,* and the three novels known as "The New York Trilogy": *City of Glass, Ghosts,* and *The Locked Room.* In nonfiction, he has written *The Invention of Solitude, The Art of Hunger,* and several books of poetry. He has twice received literary fellowships from the National Endowment for the Arts, and has received the 1990 Morton Dauwen Zabel Award from the American Academy of Arts and Letters. His work has been translated into fifteen languages. His latest novel, *The Music of Chance,* was published by Viking in the fall of 1990.

CITY OF GLASS

by Paul Auster

The New York Trilogy, volume 1

Penguin Books

PENGUIN BOOKS
Published by the Penguin Group
Viking Penguin, a division of Penguin Books USA Inc.,
375 Hudson Street, New York, New York 10014, U.S.A.
Penguin Books Ltd, 27 Wrights Lane, London W8 5TZ, England
Penguin Books Australia Ltd, Ringwood, Victoria, Australia
Penguin Books Canada Ltd, 2801 John Street,
Markham, Ontario, Canada L3R 1B4
Penguin Books (N.Z.) Ltd, 182–190 Wairau Road, Auckland 10, New Zealand

Penguin Books Ltd, Registered Offices:
Harmondsworth, Middlesex, England

First published in the United States of America by
Sun & Moon Press 1985
Published by Penguin Books 1987

7   9   10   8   6

Publication of this book was made possible, in part,
through a grant from the National Endowment for the Arts
and through contributions to
the Contemporary Arts Educational Project, Inc.

LIBRARY OF CONGRESS CATALOGING IN PUBLICATION DATA
Auster, Paul, 1947–
City of glass.
(The New York trilogy; v. l)
I. Title.   II. Series: Auster, Paul, 1947–   . New
York trilogy: v. l.
PS3551.U77C5   1987   813′.54   86-18678
ISBN 0 14 00.9731 7

Printed in the United States of America
Set in Bodoni

1

IT was a wrong number that started it, the telephone ringing three times in the dead of night, and the voice on the other end asking for someone he was not. Much later, when he was able to think about the things that happened to him, he would conclude that nothing was real except chance. But that was much later. In the beginning, there was simply the event and its consequences. Whether it might have turned out differently, or whether it was all predetermined with the first word that came from the stranger's mouth, is not the question. The question is the story itself, and whether or not it means something is not for the story to tell.

As for Quinn, there is little that need detain us. Who he was, where he came from, and what he did are of no great importance. We know, for example, that he was thirty-five years old. We know that he had once been married, had once been a father, and that both his wife and son were now dead. We also know that he wrote books. To be precise, we know that he wrote mystery novels. These works were written under the name of William Wilson, and he produced them at the rate of about one a year, which brought in enough money for him to live modestly in a small New York apartment. Because he spent no more than five or six months on a novel, for the rest of the year he was free to do as he wished. He read many books, he looked at paintings, he went to the movies. In the summer he watched baseball on television; in the winter he went to the opera. More than anything else, however, what he liked to do was walk. Nearly every day, rain or shine, hot or cold, he would leave his apartment to walk through the city—never really going anywhere, but simply going wherever his legs happened to take him.

New York was an inexhaustible space, a labyrinth of endless steps, and no matter how far he walked, no matter how well he came to know its neighborhoods and streets, it always left him with the feeling of being lost. Lost, not only in the city, but within himself as well. Each time he took a walk, he felt as though he were leaving himself behind, and by giving himself up to the movement of the streets, by reducing himself to a seeing eye, he was able to escape the obligation to think, and this, more than anything else, brought him a measure of peace, a salutary emptiness within. The world was outside of him, around him, before him, and the speed with which it kept changing made it impossible for him to dwell on any one thing for very long. Motion was of the essence, the act of putting one foot in front of the other and allowing himself to follow the drift of his own body. By wandering aimlessly, all places became equal, and it no longer mattered where he was. On his best walks, he was able to feel that he was nowhere. And this, finally, was all he ever asked of things: to be nowhere. New York was the nowhere he had built around himself, and he realized that he had no intention of ever leaving it again.

In the past, Quinn had been more ambitious. As a young man he had published several books of poetry, had written plays, critical essays, and had worked on a number of long translations. But quite abruptly, he had given up all that. A part of him had died, he told his friends, and he did not want it coming back to haunt him. It was then that he had taken on the name of William Wilson. Quinn was no longer that part of him that could write books, and although in many ways Quinn continued to exist, he no longer existed for anyone but himself.

He had continued to write because it was the only thing he felt he could do. Mystery novels seemed a reasonable solution. He had little trouble inventing the intricate stories they required, and he wrote well, often in spite of himself, as if without having to make an effort. Because he did not consider himself to be the author of what he wrote, he did not feel responsible for it and therefore was not compelled to defend it in his heart. William Wilson, after all, was an invention, and even though he had been born within Quinn himself, he now led an independent life. Quinn treated him with deference, at times even admiration, but he never went so far as to believe that he and William Wilson were the same man. It was for this reason that he did not emerge from behind the mask of his pseudonym. He had an agent, but they had never met. Their contacts were confined to the mail, for which purpose Quinn had rented a numbered box at the post office. The same was true of the publisher, who paid all fees, monies, and royalties to Quinn through the agent. No book by William Wilson ever included an author's photograph or biographical note. William Wilson was not listed in any writers' directory, he did not give interviews, and all the letters he received were answered by his agent's secretary. As far as Quinn could tell, no one knew his secret. In the beginning, when his friends learned that he had given up writing, they would ask him how he was planning to live. He told them all the same thing: that he had inherited a trust fund from his wife. But the fact was that his wife had never had any money. And the fact was that he no longer had any friends.

It had been more than five years now. He did not think about his son very much anymore, and only recently he had removed the photograph of his wife from the wall. Every once in a while, he would suddenly feel what it had been like to hold the three-year-old boy in his arms—but that was not exactly thinking, nor was it even remembering. It was a physical sensation, an imprint of the past that had been left in his body, and he had no control over it. These moments came less often now, and for the most part it seemed as though things had begun to change for him. He no longer wished to be dead. At the same time, it cannot be said that he was glad to be alive. But at least he did not resent it. He was alive, and the stubbornness of this fact had little by little begun to fascinate him—as if he had managed to outlive himself, as if he were somehow living a posthumous life. He did not sleep with the lamp on anymore, and for many months now he had not remembered any of his dreams.

It was night. Quinn lay in bed smoking a cigarette, listening to the rain beat against the window. He wondered when it would stop and whether he would feel like taking a long walk or a short walk in the morning. An open copy of Marco Polo's *Travels* lay face down on the pillow beside him. Since finishing the latest William Wilson novel two weeks earlier, he had been languishing. His private-eye narrator, Max Work, had solved an elaborate series of crimes, had suffered through a number of beatings and narrow escapes, and Quinn was feeling somewhat exhausted by his efforts. Over the years, Work had become very close to Quinn. Whereas William Wilson remained an abstract figure for him, Work had increasingly come to life. In the triad of selves that Quinn had become, Wilson served as a kind of ventriloquist, Quinn himself was the dummy, and Work was the animated voice that gave purpose to the enterprise. If Wilson was an illusion, he nevertheless justified the lives of the other two. If Wilson did not exist, he nevertheless was the bridge that allowed Quinn to pass from himself into Work. And little by little, Work had become a presence in Quinn's life, his interior brother, his comrade in solitude.

Quinn picked up the Marco Polo and started reading the first page again. "We will set down things seen as seen, things heard as heard, so that our book may be an accurate record, free from any sort of fabrication. And all who read this book or hear it may do so with full confidence, because it contains nothing but the truth." Just as Quinn was beginning to ponder the meaning of these sentences, to turn their crisp assurances over in his mind, the telephone rang. Much later, when he was able to reconstruct the events of that night, he would remember looking at the clock, seeing that it was past twelve, and wondering why someone should be calling him at that hour. More than likely, he thought, it was bad news. He climbed out of bed, walked naked to the telephone, and picked up the receiver on the second ring.

"Yes?"

There was a long pause on the other end, and for a moment Quinn thought the caller had hung up. Then, as if from a great distance, there came the sound of a voice unlike any he had ever heard. It was at once mechanical and filled with feeling, hardly more than a whisper and yet perfectly audible, and so even in tone that he was unable to tell if it belonged to a man or a woman.

"Hello?" said the voice.

"Who is this?" asked Quinn.

"Hello?" said the voice again.

"I'm listening," said Quinn. "Who is this?"

"Is this Paul Auster?" asked the voice. "I would like to speak to Mr. Paul Auster."

"There's no one here by that name."

"Paul Auster. Of the Auster Detective Agency."

"I'm sorry," said Quinn. "You must have the wrong number."

"This is a matter of utmost urgency," said the voice.

"There's nothing I can do for you," said Quinn. "There is no Paul Auster here."

"You don't understand," said the voice. "Time is running out."

"Then I suggest you dial again. This is not a detective agency."

Quinn hung up the phone. He stood there on the cold floor, looking down at his feet, his knees, his limp penis. For a brief moment he regretted having been so abrupt with the caller. It might have been interesting, he thought, to have played along with him a little. Perhaps he could have found out something about the case—perhaps even have helped in some way. "I must learn to think more quickly on my feet," he said to himself.

Like most people, Quinn knew almost nothing about crime. He had never murdered anyone, had never stolen anything, and he did not know anyone who had. He had never been inside a police station, had never met a private detective, had never spoken to a criminal. Whatever he knew about these things, he had learned from books, films, and newspapers. He did not, however, consider this to be a handicap. What interested him about the stories he wrote was not their relation to the world but their relation to other stories. Even before he became William Wilson, Quinn had been a devoted reader of mystery novels. He knew that most of them were poorly written, that most could not stand up to even the vaguest sort of examination, but still, it was the form that appealed to him, and it was the rare, unspeakably bad mystery that he would refuse to read. Whereas his taste in other books was rigorous, demanding to the point of narrow-mindedness, with these works he showed almost no discrimination whatsoever. When he was in the right mood, he had little trouble reading ten or twelve of them in a row. It was a kind of hunger that took hold of him, a craving for a special food, and he would not stop until he had eaten his fill.

What he liked about these books was their sense of

plenitude and economy. In the good mystery there is nothing wasted, no sentence, no word that is not significant. And even if it is not significant, it has the potential to be so—which amounts to the same thing. The world of the book comes to life, seething with possibilities, with secrets and contradictions. Since everything seen or said, even the slightest, most trivial thing, can bear a connection to the outcome of the story, nothing must be overlooked. Everything becomes essence; the center of the book shifts with each event that propels it forward. The center, then, is everywhere, and no circumference can be drawn until the book has come to its end.

The detective is one who looks, who listens, who moves through this morass of objects and events in search of the thought, the idea that will pull all these things together and make sense of them. In effect, the writer and the detective are interchangeable. The reader sees the world through the detective's eyes, experiencing the proliferation of its details as if for the first time. He has become awake to the things around him, as if they might speak to him, as if, because of the attentiveness he now brings to them, they might begin to carry a meaning other than the simple fact of their existence. Private eye. The term held a triple meaning for Quinn. Not only was it the letter "i," standing for "investigator," it was "I" in the upper case, the tiny life-bud buried in the body of the breathing self. At the same time, it was also the physical eye of the writer, the eye of the man who looks out from himself into the world and demands that the world reveal itself to him. For five years now, Quinn had been living in the grip of this pun.

He had, of course, long ago stopped thinking of himself as real. If he lived now in the world at all, it was only at one remove, through the imaginary person of Max Work. His detective necessarily had to be real. The nature of the books demanded it. If Quinn had allowed himself to vanish, to withdraw into the confines of a strange and hermetic life, Work continued to live in the world of others, and the more Quinn seemed to vanish, the more persistent Work's presence in that world became. Whereas Quinn tended to feel out of place in his own skin, Work was aggressive, quick-tongued, at home in whatever spot he happened to find himself. The very things that caused problems for Quinn, Work took for granted, and he walked through the mayhem of his adventures with an ease and indifference that never failed to impress his creator. It was not precisely that Quinn wanted to be Work, or even to be like him, but it reassured him to pretend to be Work as he was writing his books, to know that he had it in him to be Work if he ever chose to be, even if only in his mind.

That night, as he at last drifted off to sleep, Quinn tried to imagine what Work would have said to the stranger on the phone. In his dream, which he later forgot, he found himself alone in a room, firing a pistol into a bare white wall.

The following night, Quinn was caught off guard. He had thought the incident was over and was not expecting the stranger to call again. As it happened, he was sitting on the toilet, in the act of expelling a turd, when the telephone rang. It was somewhat later than the previous night, perhaps ten or twelve minutes before one. Quinn had just reached the chapter that tells of Marco Polo's journey from Peking to Amoy, and the book was open on his lap as he went about his business in the tiny bathroom. The ringing of the telephone came as a distinct irritation. To answer it promptly would mean getting up without wiping himself, and he was loath to walk across the apartment in that state. On the other hand, if he finished what he was doing at his normal speed, he would not make it to the phone in time. In spite of this, Quinn found himself reluctant to move. The telephone was not his favorite object, and more than once he had considered getting rid of his. What he disliked most of all was its tyranny. Not only did it have the power to interrupt him against his will, but inevitably he would give in to its command. This time, he decided to resist. By the third ring, his bowels were empty. By the fourth ring, he had succeeded in wiping himself. By the fifth ring, he had pulled up his pants, left the bathroom, and was walking calmly across the apartment. He answered the phone on the sixth ring, but there was no one at the other end. The caller had hung up.

The next night, he was ready. Sprawled out on his bed,

perusing the pages of *The Sporting News*, he waited for the stranger to call a third time. Every now and then, when his nerves got the better of him, he would stand up and pace about the apartment. He put on a record—Haydn's opera *The World on the Moon*—and listened to it from start to finish. He waited and waited. At two-thirty, he finally gave up and went to sleep.

He waited the next night, and the night after that as well. Just as he was about to abandon his scheme, realizing that he had been wrong in all his assumptions, the telephone rang again. It was May nineteenth. He would remember the date because it was his parents' anniversary— or would have been, had his parents been alive—and his mother had once told him that he had been conceived on her wedding night. This fact had always appealed to him— being able to pinpoint the first moment of his existence— and over the years he had privately celebrated his birthday on that day. This time it was somewhat earlier than on the other two nights—not yet eleven o'clock—and as he reached for the phone he assumed it was someone else.

"Hello?" he said.

Again, there was a silence on the other end. Quinn knew at once that it was the stranger.

"Hello?" he said again. "What can I do for you?"

"Yes," said the voice at last. The same mechanical whisper, the same desperate tone. "Yes. It is needed now. Without delay."

"What is needed?"

"To speak. Right now. To speak right now. Yes."

"And who do you want to speak to?"

"Always the same man. Auster. The one who calls himself Paul Auster."

This time Quinn did not hesitate. He knew what he was going to do, and now that the time had come, he did it.

"Speaking," he said. "This is Auster speaking."

"At last. At last I've found you." He could hear the relief in the voice, the tangible calm that suddenly seemed to overtake it.

"That's right," said Quinn. "At last." He paused for a moment to let the words sink in, as much for himself as for the other. "What can I do for you?"

"I need help," said the voice. "There is great danger. They say you are the best one to do these things."

"It depends on what things you mean."

"I mean death. I mean death and murder."

"That's not exactly my line," said Quinn. "I don't go around killing people."

"No," said the voice petulantly. "I mean the reverse."

"Someone is going to kill you?"

"Yes, kill me. That's right. I am going to be murdered."

"And you want me to protect you?"

"To protect me, yes. And to find the man who is going to do it."

"You don't know who it is?"

"I know, yes. Of course I know. But I don't know where he is."

"Can you tell me about it?"

"Not now. Not on the phone. There is great danger. You must come here."

"How about tomorrow?"

"Good. Tomorrow. Early tomorrow. In the morning."

"Ten o'clock?"

"Good. Ten o'clock." The voice gave an address on East 69th Street. "Don't forget, Mr. Auster. You must come."

"Don't worry," said Quinn. "I'll be there."

———————————

2

THE next morning, Quinn woke up earlier than he had in several weeks. As he drank his coffee, buttered his toast, and read through the baseball scores in the paper (the Mets had lost again, two to one, on a ninth inning error), it did not occur to him that he was going to show up for his appointment. Even that locution, *his appointment*, seemed odd to him. It wasn't his appointment, it was Paul Auster's. And who that person was he had no idea.

Nevertheless, as time wore on he found himself doing a good imitation of a man preparing to go out. He cleared the table of the breakfast dishes, tossed the newspaper on the couch, went into the bathroom, showered, shaved, went on to the bedroom wrapped in two towels, opened the closet, and picked out his clothes for the day. He found himself tending toward a jacket and tie. Quinn had not worn a tie since the funerals of his wife and son, and he could not even remember if he still owned one. But there it was, hanging amidst the debris of his wardrobe. He dismissed a white shirt as too formal, however, and instead chose a gray and red check affair to go with the gray tie. He put them on in a kind of trance.

It was not until he had his hand on the doorknob that he began to suspect what he was doing. "I seem to be going out," he said to himself. "But if I am going out, where exactly am I going?" An hour later, as he climbed from the number 4 bus at 70th Street and Fifth Avenue, he still had not answered the question. To one side of him was the park, green in the morning sun, with sharp, fleeting shadows; to the other side was the Frick, white and austere, as if abandoned to the dead. He thought for a moment of Vermeer's *Soldier and Young Girl Smiling*, trying to remember the expression on the girl's face, the exact position of her hands around the cup, the red back of the faceless man. In his mind, he caught a glimpse of the blue map on the wall and the sunlight pouring through the window, so like the sunlight that surrounded him now. He was walking. He was crossing the street and moving eastward. At Madison Avenue he turned right and went south for a block, then turned left and saw where he was. "I seem to have arrived," he said to himself. He stood before the building and paused. It suddenly did not seem to matter anymore. He felt remarkably calm, as if everything had already happened to him. As he opened the door that would lead him into the lobby, he gave himself one last word of advice. "If all this is really happening," he said, "then I must keep my eyes open."

●

It was a woman who opened the apartment door. For
some reason, Quinn had not been expecting this, and it
threw him off track. Already, things were happening too
fast. Before he had a chance to absorb the woman's presence, to describe her to himself and form his impressions,
she was talking to him, forcing him to respond. Therefore,
even in those first moments, he had lost ground, was starting to fall behind himself. Later, when he had time to
reflect on these events, he would manage to piece together
his encounter with the woman. But that was the work of
memory, and remembered things, he knew, had a tendency
to subvert the things remembered. As a consequence, he
could never be sure of any of it.

The woman was thirty, perhaps thirty-five; average height
at best; hips a touch wide, or else voluptuous, depending
on your point of view; dark hair, dark eyes, and a look in
those eyes that was at once self-contained and vaguely
seductive. She wore a black dress and very red lipstick.

"Mr. Auster?" A tentative smile; a questioning tilt to
the head.

"That's right," said Quinn. "Paul Auster."

"I'm Virginia Stillman," the woman began. "Peter's wife.
He's been waiting for you since eight o'clock."

"The appointment was for ten," said Quinn, glancing at
his watch. It was exactly ten.

"He's been frantic," the woman explained. "I've never
seen him like this before. He just couldn't wait."

She opened the door for Quinn. As he crossed the threshold and entered the apartment, he could feel himself going blank, as if his brain had suddenly shut off. He had wanted to take in the details of what he was seeing, but the task was somehow beyond him at that moment. The apartment loomed up around him as a kind of blur. He realized that it was large, perhaps five or six rooms, and that it was richly furnished, with numerous art objects, silver ashtrays, and elaborately framed paintings on the walls. But that was all. No more than a general impression—even though he was there, looking at those things with his own eyes.

He found himself sitting on a sofa, alone in the living room. He remembered now that Mrs. Stillman had told him to wait there while she went to find her husband. He couldn't say how long it had been. Surely no more than a minute or two. But from the way the light was coming through the windows, it seemed to be almost noon. It did not occur to him, however, to consult his watch. The smell of Virginia Stillman's perfume hovered around him, and he began to imagine what she looked like without any clothes on. Then he thought about what Max Work might have been thinking, had he been there. He decided to light a cigarette. He blew the smoke into the room. It pleased him to watch it leave his mouth in gusts, disperse, and take on new definition as the light caught it.

He heard the sound of someone entering the room behind

him. Quinn stood up from the sofa and turned around, expecting to see Mrs. Stillman. Instead, it was a young man, dressed entirely in white, with the white-blond hair of a child. Uncannily, in that first moment, Quinn thought of his own dead son. Then, just as suddenly as the thought had appeared, it vanished.

Peter Stillman walked into the room and sat down in a red velvet armchair opposite Quinn. He said not a word as he made his way to his seat, nor did he acknowledge Quinn's presence. The act of moving from one place to another seemed to require all his attention, as though not to think of what he was doing would reduce him to immobility. Quinn had never seen anyone move in such a manner, and he realized at once that this was the same person he had spoken to on the phone. The body acted almost exactly as the voice had: machine-like, fitful, alternating between slow and rapid gestures, rigid and yet expressive, as if the operation were out of control, not quite corresponding to the will that lay behind it. It seemed to Quinn that Stillman's body had not been used for a long time and that all its functions had been relearned, so that motion had become a conscious process, each movement broken down into its component submovements, with the result that all flow and spontaneity had been lost. It was like watching a marionette trying to walk without strings.

Everything about Peter Stillman was white. White shirt, open at the neck; white pants, white shoes, white socks.

Against the pallor of his skin, the flaxen thinness of his hair, the effect was almost transparent, as though one could see through to the blue veins behind the skin of his face. This blue was almost the same as the blue of his eyes: a milky blue that seemed to dissolve into a mixture of sky and clouds. Quinn could not imagine himself addressing a word to this person. It was as though Stillman's presence was a command to be silent.

Stillman settled slowly into his chair and at last turned his attention to Quinn. As their eyes met, Quinn suddenly felt that Stillman had become invisible. He could see him sitting in the chair across from him, but at the same time it felt as though he was not there. It occurred to Quinn that perhaps Stillman was blind. But no, that did not seem possible. The man was looking at him, even studying him, and if recognition did not flicker across his face, it still held something more than a blank stare. Quinn did not know what to do. He sat there dumbly in his seat, looking back at Stillman. A long time passed.

"No questions, please," the young man said at last. "Yes. No. Thank you." He paused for a moment. "I am Peter Stillman. I say this of my own free will. Yes. That is not my real name. No. Of course, my mind is not all it should be. But nothing can be done about that. No. About that. No, no. Not anymore.

"You sit there and think: who is this person talking to me? What are these words coming from his mouth? I will tell you. Or else I will not tell you. Yes and no. My mind is not all it should be. I say this of my own free will. But I will try. Yes and no. I will try to tell you, even if my mind makes it hard. Thank you.

"My name is Peter Stillman. Perhaps you have heard of me, but more than likely not. No matter. That is not my real name. My real name I cannot remember. Excuse me. Not that it makes a difference. That is to say, anymore.

"This is what is called speaking. I believe that is the term. When words come out, fly into the air, live for a moment, and die. Strange, is it not? I myself have no opinion. No and no again. But still, there are words you will need to have. There are many of them. Many millions, I think. Perhaps only three or four. Excuse me. But I am doing well today. So much better than usual. If I can give you the words you need to have, it will be a great victory. Thank you. Thank you a million times over.

"Long ago there was mother and father. I remember none of that. They say: mother died. Who they are I cannot say. Excuse me. But that is what they say.

"No mother, then. Ha ha. Such is my laughter now, my belly burst of mumbo jumbo. Ha ha ha. Big father said: it makes no difference. To me. That is to say, to him. Big father of the big muscles and the boom, boom, boom. No questions now, please.

"I say what they say because I know nothing. I am only poor Peter Stillman, the boy who can't remember. Boo hoo.

Willy nilly. Nincompoop. Excuse me. They say, they say. But what does poor little Peter say? Nothing, nothing. Anymore.

"There was this. Dark. Very dark. As dark as very dark. They say: that was the room. As if I could talk about it. The dark, I mean. Thank you.

"Dark, dark. They say for nine years. Not even a window. Poor Peter Stillman. And the boom, boom, boom. The caca piles. The pipi lakes. The swoons. Excuse me. Numb and naked. Excuse me. Anymore.

"There is the dark then. I am telling you. There was food in the dark, yes, mush food in the hush dark room. He ate with his hands. Excuse me. I mean Peter did. And if I am Peter, so much the better. That is to say, so much the worse. Excuse me. I am Peter Stillman. That is not my real name. Thank you.

"Poor Peter Stillman. A little boy he was. Barely a few words of his own. And then no words, and then no one, and then no, no, no. Anymore.

"Forgive me, Mr. Auster. I see that I am making you sad. No questions, please. My name is Peter Stillman. That is not my real name. My real name is Mr. Sad. What is your name, Mr. Auster? Perhaps you are the real Mr. Sad, and I am no one.

"Boo hoo. Excuse me. Such is my weeping and wailing. Boo hoo, sob sob. What did Peter do in that room? No one can say. Some say nothing. As for me, I think that Peter could not think. Did he blink? Did he drink? Did he stink? Ha ha ha. Excuse me. Sometimes I am so funny.

"Wimble click crumblechaw beloo. Clack clack bedrack. Numb noise, flacklemuch, chewmanna. Ya, ya, ya. Excuse me. I am the only one who understands these words.

"Later and later and later. So they say. It went on too long for Peter to be right in the head. Never again. No, no, no. They say that someone found me. I do not remember. No, I do not remember what happened when they opened the door and the light came in. No, no, no. I can say nothing about any of this. Anymore.

"For a long time I wore dark glasses. I was twelve. Or so they say. I lived in a hospital. Little by little, they taught me how to be Peter Stillman. They said: you are Peter Stillman. Thank you, I said. Ya, ya, ya. Thank you and thank you, I said.

"Peter was a baby. They had to teach him everything. How to walk, you know. How to eat. How to make caca and pipi in the toilet. That wasn't bad. Even when I bit them, they didn't do the boom, boom, boom. Later, I even stopped tearing off my clothes.

"Peter was a good boy. But it was hard to teach him words. His mouth did not work right. And of course he was not all there in his head. Ba ba ba, he said. And da da da. And wa wa wa. Excuse me. It took more years and years. Now they say to Peter: you can go now, there's nothing more we can do for you. Peter Stillman, you are a human being, they said. It is good to believe what doctors say. Thank you. Thank you so very much.

"I am Peter Stillman. That is not my real name. My real name is Peter Rabbit. In the winter I am Mr. White, in the summer I am Mr. Green. Think what you like of this. I say it of my own free will. Wimble click crumblechaw beloo. It is beautiful, is it not? I make up words like this all the time. That can't be helped. They just come out of my mouth by themselves. They cannot be translated.

"Ask and ask. It does no good. But I will tell you. I don't want you to be sad, Mr. Auster. You have such a kind face. You remind me of a somesuch or a groan, I don't know which. And your eyes look at me. Yes, yes. I can see them. That is very good. Thank you.

"That is why I will tell you. No questions, please. You are wondering about all the rest. That is to say, the father. The terrible father who did all those things to little Peter. Rest assured. They took him to a dark place. They locked him up and left him there. Ha ha ha. Excuse me. Sometimes I am so funny.

"Thirteen years, they said. That is perhaps a long time. But I know nothing of time. I am new every day. I am born when I wake up in the morning, I grow old during the day, and I die at night when I go to sleep. It is not my fault. I am doing so well today. I am doing so much better than I have ever done before.

"For thirteen years the father was away. His name is Peter Stillman too. Strange, is it not? That two people can have the same name? I do not know if that is his real name. But I do not think he is me. We are both Peter Stillman. But Peter Stillman is not my real name. So perhaps I am not Peter Stillman, after all.

"Thirteen years I say. Or they say. It makes no difference. I know nothing of time. But what they tell me is this. Tomorrow is the end of thirteen years. That is bad. Even though they say it is not, it is bad. I am not supposed to remember. But now and then I do, in spite of what I say.

"He will come. That is to say, the father will come. And he will try to kill me. Thank you. But I do not want that. No, no. Not anymore. Peter lives now. Yes. All is not right in his head, but still he lives. And that is something, is it not? You bet your bottom dollar. Ha ha ha.

"I am mostly now a poet. Every day I sit in my room and write another poem. I make up all the words myself, just like when I lived in the dark. I begin to remember things that way, to pretend that I am back in the dark again. I am the only one who knows what the words mean. They cannot be translated. These poems will make me famous. Hit the nail on the head. Ya, ya, ya. Beautiful poems. So beautiful the whole world will weep.

"Later perhaps I will do something else. After I am done being a poet. Sooner or later I will run out of words, you

see. Everyone has just so many words inside him. And
then where will I be? I think I would like to be a fireman
after that. And after that a doctor. It makes no difference.
The last thing I will be is a high-wire walker. When I am
very old and have at last learned how to walk like other
people. Then I will dance on the wire, and people will be
amazed. Even little children. That is what I would like.
To dance on the wire until I die.

"But no matter. It makes no difference. To me. As you
can see, I am a rich man. I do not have to worry. No, no.
Not about that. You bet your bottom dollar. The father was
rich, and little Peter got all his money after they locked
him up in the dark. Ha ha ha. Excuse me for laughing.
Sometimes I am so funny.

"I am the last of the Stillmans. That was quite a family,
or so they say. From old Boston, in case you might have
heard of it. I am the last one. There are no others. I am
the end of everyone, the last man. So much the better, I
think. It is not a pity that it should all end now. It is good
for everyone to be dead.

"The father was perhaps not really bad. At least I say
so now. He had a big head. As big as very big, which
meant there was too much room in there. So many thoughts
in that big head of his. But poor Peter, was he not? And
in terrible straits indeed. Peter who could not see or say,
who could not think or do. Peter who could not. No. Not
anything.

"I know nothing of any of this. Nor do I understand. My wife is the one who tells me these things. She says it is important for me to know, even if I do not understand. But even this I do not understand. In order to know, you must understand. Is that not so? But I know nothing. Perhaps I am Peter Stillman, and perhaps I am not. My real name is Peter Nobody. Thank you. And what do you think of that?

"So I am telling you about the father. It is a good story, even if I do not understand it. I can tell it to you because I know the words. And that is something, is it not? To know the words, I mean. Sometimes I am so proud of myself! Excuse me. This is what my wife says. She says the father talked about God. That is a funny word to me. When you put it backwards, it spells dog. And a dog is not much like God, is it? Woof woof. Bow wow. Those are dog words. I think they are beautiful. So pretty and true. Like the words I make up.

"Anyway. I was saying. The father talked about God. He wanted to know if God had a language. Don't ask me what this means. I am only telling you because I know the words. The father thought a baby might speak it if the baby saw no people. But what baby was there? Ah. Now you begin to see. You did not have to buy him. Of course, Peter knew some people words. That could not be helped. But the father thought maybe Peter would forget them. After a while. That is why there was so much boom, boom,

boom. Every time Peter said a word, his father would boom him. At last Peter learned to say nothing. Ya ya ya. Thank you.

"Peter kept the words inside him. All those days and months and years. There in the dark, little Peter all alone, and the words made noise in his head and kept him company. That is why his mouth does not work right. Poor Peter. Boo hoo. Such are his tears. The little boy who can never grow up.

"Peter can talk like people now. But he still has the other words in his head. They are God's language, and no one else can speak them. They cannot be translated. That is why Peter lives so close to God. That is why he is a famous poet.

"Everything is so good for me now. I can do whatever I like. Any time, any place. I even have a wife. You can see that. I mentioned her before. Perhaps you have even met her. She is beautiful, is she not? Her name is Virginia. That is not her real name. But that makes no difference. To me.

"Whenever I ask, my wife gets a girl for me. They are whores. I put my worm inside them and they moan. There have been so many. Ha ha. They come up here and I fuck them. It feels good to fuck. Virginia gives them money and everyone is happy. You bet your bottom dollar. Ha ha.

"Poor Virginia. She does not like to fuck. That is to

say, with me. Perhaps she fucks another. Who can say? I know nothing of this. It makes no difference. But maybe if you are nice to Virginia she will let you fuck her. It would make me happy. For your sake. Thank you.

"So. There are a great many things. I am trying to tell them to you. I know that all is not right in my head. And it is true, yes, and I say this of my own free will, that sometimes I just scream and scream. For no good reason. As if there had to be a reason. But for none that I can see. Or anyone else. No. And then there are the times when I say nothing. For days and days on end. Nothing, nothing, nothing. I forget how to make the words come out of my mouth. Then it is hard for me to move. Ya ya. Or even to see. That is when I become Mr. Sad.

"I still like to be in the dark. At least sometimes. It does me good, I think. In the dark I speak God's language and no one can hear me. Do not be angry, please. I cannot help it.

"Best of all, there is the air. Yes. And little by little, I have learned to live inside it. The air and the light, yes, that too, the light that shines on all things and puts them there for my eyes to see. There is the air and the light, and this best of all. Excuse me. The air and the light. Yes. When the weather is good, I like to sit by the open window. Sometimes I look out and watch the things below. The street and all the people, the dogs and cars, the bricks of the building across the way. And then there are the times when I close my eyes and just sit there, with the breeze blowing on my face, and the light inside the air, all around me and just beyond my eyes, and the world all red, a beautiful red inside my eyes, with the sun shining on me and my eyes.

"It is true that I rarely go out. It is hard for me, and I am not always to be trusted. Sometimes I scream. Do not be angry with me, please. I cannot help it. Virginia says I must learn how to behave in public. But sometimes I cannot help myself, and the screams just come out of me.

"But I do love going to the park. There are the trees, and the air and the light. There is good in all that, is there not? Yes. Little by little, I am getting better inside myself. I can feel it. Even Dr. Wyshnegradsky says so. I know that I am still the puppet boy. That cannot be helped. No, no. Anymore. But sometimes I think I will at last grow up and become real.

"For now, I am still Peter Stillman. That is not my real name. I cannot say who I will be tomorrow. Each day is new, and each day I am born again. I see hope everywhere, even in the dark, and when I die I will perhaps become God.

"There are many more words to speak. But I do not think I will speak them. No. Not today. My mouth is tired now, and I think the time has come for me to go. Of course, I know nothing of time. But that makes no difference. To me. Thank you very much. I know you will save my life,

Mr. Auster. I am counting on you. Life can last just so long, you understand. Everything else is in the room, with darkness, with God's language, with screams. Here I am of the air, a beautiful thing for the light to shine on. Perhaps you will remember that. I am Peter Stillman. That is not my real name. Thank you very much."

3

THE speech was over. How long it had lasted Quinn
could not say. For it was only now, after the words
had stopped, that he realized they were sitting in the dark.
Apparently, a whole day had gone by. At some point during
Stillman's monologue the sun had set in the room, but
Quinn had not been aware of it. Now he could feel the
darkness and the silence, and his head was humming with
them. Several minutes went by. Quinn thought that perhaps
it was up to him to say something now, but he could not
be sure. He could hear Peter Stillman breathing heavily
in his spot across the room. Other than that, there were
no sounds. Quinn could not decide what to do. He thought
of several possibilities, but then, one by one, dismissed
them from his mind. He sat there in his seat, waiting for
the next thing to happen.

The sound of stockinged legs moving across the room
finally broke the silence. There was the metal click of a
lamp switch, and suddenly the room was filled with light.
Quinn's eyes automatically turned to its source, and there,
standing beside a table lamp to the left of Peter's chair,

he saw Virginia Stillman. The young man was gazing straight ahead, as if asleep with his eyes open. Mrs. Stillman bent over, put her arm around Peter's shoulder, and spoke softly into his ear.

"It's time now, Peter," she said. "Mrs. Saavedra is waiting for you."

Peter looked up at her and smiled. "I am filled with hope," he said.

Virginia Stillman kissed her husband tenderly on the cheek. "Say good-bye to Mr. Auster," she said.

Peter stood up. Or rather, he began the sad, slow adventure of maneuvering his body out of the chair and working his way to his feet. At each stage there were relapses, crumplings, catapults back, accompanied by sudden fits of immobility, grunts, words whose meaning Quinn could not decipher.

At last Peter was upright. He stood in front of his chair with an expression of triumph and looked Quinn in the eyes. Then he smiled, broadly and without self-consciousness.

"Good-bye," he said.

"Good-bye, Peter," said Quinn.

Peter gave a little spastic wave of the hand and then slowly turned and walked across the room. He tottered as he went, listing first to the right, then to the left, his legs by turns buckling and locking. At the far end of the room, standing in a lighted doorway, was a middle-aged woman dressed in a white nurse's uniform. Quinn assumed it was Mrs. Saavedra. He followed Peter Stillman with his eyes until the young man disappeared through the door.

Virginia Stillman sat down across from Quinn, in the same chair her husband had just occupied.

"I could have spared you all that," she said, "but I thought it would be best for you to see it with your own eyes."

"I understand," said Quinn.

"No, I don't think you do," the woman said bitterly. "I don't think anyone can understand."

Quinn smiled judiciously and then told himself to plunge in. "Whatever I do or do not understand," he said, "is probably beside the point. You've hired me to do a job, and the sooner I get on with it the better. From what I can gather, the case is urgent. I make no claims about understanding Peter or what you might have suffered. The important thing is that I'm willing to help. I think you should take it for what it's worth."

He was warming up now. Something told him that he had captured the right tone, and a sudden sense of pleasure surged through him, as though he had just managed to cross some internal border within himself.

"You're right," said Virginia Stillman. "Of course you're right."

The woman paused, took a deep breath, and then paused again, as if rehearsing in her mind the things she was about to say. Quinn noticed that her hands were clenched tightly around the arms of the chair.

"I realize," she went on, "that most of what Peter says is very confusing—especially the first time you hear him. I was standing in the next room listening to what he said to you. You mustn't assume that Peter always tells the truth. On the other hand, it would be wrong to think he lies."

"You mean that I should believe some of the things he said and not believe others."

"That's exactly what I mean."

"Your sexual habits, or lack of them, don't concern me, Mrs. Stillman," said Quinn. "Even if what Peter said is true, it makes no difference. In my line of work you tend to meet a little of everything, and if you don't learn to suspend judgment, you'll never get anywhere. I'm used to hearing people's secrets, and I'm also used to keeping my mouth shut. If a fact has no direct bearing on a case, I have no use for it."

Mrs. Stillman blushed. "I just wanted you to know that what Peter said isn't true."

Quinn shrugged, took out a cigarette, and lit it. "One way or the other," he said, "it's not important. What I'm interested in are the other things Peter said. I assume they're true, and if they are, I'd like to hear what you have to say about them."

"Yes, they're true." Virginia Stillman released her grip

on the chair and put her right hand under her chin. Pensive. As if searching for an attitude of unshakable honesty. "Peter has a child's way of telling it. But what he said is true."

"Tell me something about the father. Anything you think is relevant."

"Peter's father is a Boston Stillman. I'm sure you've heard of the family. There were several governors back in the nineteenth century, a number of Episcopal bishops, ambassadors, a Harvard president. At the same time, the family made a great deal of money in textiles, shipping, and God knows what else. The details are unimportant. Just so long as you have some idea of the background.

"Peter's father went to Harvard, like everyone else in the family. He studied philosophy and religion and by all accounts was quite brilliant. He wrote his thesis on sixteenth- and seventeenth-century theological interpretations of the New World, and then he took a job in the religion department at Columbia. Not long after that, he married Peter's mother. I don't know much about her. From the photographs I've seen, she was very pretty. But delicate— a little like Peter, with those pale blue eyes and white skin. When Peter was born a few years later, the family was living in a large apartment on Riverside Drive. Stillman's academic career was prospering. He rewrote his dissertation and turned it into a book—it did very well— and was made a full professor when he was thirty-four or thirty-five. Then Peter's mother died. Everything about that death is unclear. Stillman claimed that she had died in her sleep, but the evidence seemed to point to suicide. Something to do with an overdose of pills, but of course nothing could be proved. There was even some talk that he had killed her. But those were just rumors, and nothing ever came of it. The whole affair was kept very quiet.

"Peter was just two at the time, a perfectly normal child. After his wife's death, Stillman apparently had little to do with him. A nurse was hired, and for the next six months or so she took complete care of Peter. Then, out of the blue, Stillman fired her. I forget her name—a Miss Barber, I think—but she testified at the trial. It seems that Stillman just came home one day and told her that he was taking charge of Peter's upbringing. He sent in his resignation to Columbia and told them he was leaving the university to devote himself full-time to his son. Money, of course, was no object, and there was nothing anyone could do about it.

"After that, he more or less dropped out of sight. He stayed on in the same apartment, but he hardly ever went out. No one really knows what happened. I think, probably, that he began to believe in some of the far-fetched religious ideas he had written about. It made him crazy, absolutely insane. There's no other way to describe it. He locked Peter in a room in the apartment, covered up the windows, and kept him there for nine years. Try to imagine it, Mr. Auster. Nine years. An entire childhood spent in darkness, isolated from the world, with no human contact except an occasional beating. I live with the results of that experiment, and I can tell you the damage was monstrous. What you saw today was Peter at his best. It's taken thirteen years to get him this far, and I'll be damned if I let anyone hurt him again."

Mrs. Stillman stopped to catch her breath. Quinn sensed that she was on the verge of a scene and that one more word might put her over the edge. He had to speak now, or the conversation would run away from him.

"How was Peter finally discovered?" he asked.

Some of the tension went out of the woman. She exhaled audibly and looked Quinn in the eyes.

"There was a fire," she said.

"An accidental fire or one set on purpose?"

"No one knows."

"What do you think?"

"I think Stillman was in his study. He kept the records of his experiment there, and I think he finally realized that his work had been a failure. I'm not saying that he regretted anything he had done. But even taking it on his own terms, he knew he had failed. I think he reached some point of final disgust with himself that night and decided to burn his papers. But the fire got out of control, and much of

the apartment burned. Luckily, Peter's room was at the
other end of a long hall, and the firemen got to him in
time."

"And then?"

"It took several months to sort everything out. Stillman's
papers had been destroyed, which meant there was no
concrete evidence. On the other hand, there was Peter's
condition, the room he had been locked up in, those hor-
rible boards across the windows, and eventually the police
put the case together. Stillman was finally brought to trial."

"What happened in court?"

"Stillman was judged insane and he was sent away."

"And Peter?"

"He also went to a hospital. He stayed there until just
two years ago."

"Is that where you met him?"

"Yes. In the hospital."

"How?"

"I was his speech therapist. I worked with Peter every
day for five years."

"I don't mean to pry. But how exactly did that lead to
marriage?"

"It's complicated."

"Do you mind telling me about it?"

"Not really. But I don't think you'd understand."

"There's only one way to find out."

"Well, to put it simply. It was the best way to get Peter

out of the hospital and give him a chance to lead a more normal life."

"Couldn't you have been made his legal guardian?"

"The procedures were very complicated. And besides, Peter was no longer a minor."

"Wasn't that an enormous self-sacrifice on your part?"

"Not really. I was married once before—disastrously. It's not something I want for myself anymore. At least with Peter there's a purpose to my life."

"Is it true that Stillman is being released?"

"Tomorrow. He'll be arriving at Grand Central in the evening."

"And you feel he might come after Peter. Is this just a hunch, or do you have some proof?"

"A little of both. Two years ago, they were going to let Stillman out. But he wrote Peter a letter, and I showed it to the authorities. They decided he wasn't ready to be released, after all."

"What kind of letter was it?"

"An insane letter. He called Peter a devil boy and said there would be a day of reckoning."

"Do you still have the letter?"

"No. I gave it to the police two years ago."

"A copy?"

"I'm sorry. Do you think it's important?"

"It might be."

"I can try to get one for you if you like."

"I take it there were no more letters after that one."

"No more letters. And now they feel Stillman is ready to be discharged. That's the official view, in any case, and there's nothing I can do to stop them. What I think, though, is that Stillman simply learned his lesson. He realized that letters and threats would keep him locked up."

"And so you're still worried."

"That's right."

"But you have no precise idea of what Stillman's plans might be."

"Exactly."

"What is it you want me to do?"

"I want you to watch him carefully. I want you to find out what he's up to. I want you to keep him away from Peter."

"In other words, a kind of glorified tail job."

"I suppose so."

"I think you should understand that I can't prevent Stillman from coming to this building. What I can do is warn you about it. And I can make it my business to come here with him."

"I understand. As long as there's some protection."

"Good. How often do you want me to check in with you?"

"I'd like you to give me a report every day. Say a telephone call in the evening, around ten or eleven o'clock."

"No problem."

"Is there anything else."

"Just a few more questions. I'm curious, for example, to know how you found out that Stillman will be coming into Grand Central tomorrow evening."

"I've made it my business to know, Mr. Auster. There's too much at stake here for me to leave it to chance. And if Stillman isn't followed from the moment he arrives, he could easily disappear without a trace. I don't want that to happen."

"Which train will he be on?"

"The six-forty-one, arriving from Poughkeepsie."

"I assume you have a photograph of Stillman?"

"Yes, of course."

"There's also the question of Peter. I'd like to know why you told him about all this in the first place. Wouldn't it have been better to have kept it quiet?"

"I wanted to. But Peter happened to be listening in on the other phone when I got the news of his father's release. There was nothing I could do about it. Peter can be very stubborn, and I've learned it's best not to lie to him."

"One last question. Who was it who referred you to me?"

"Mrs. Saavedra's husband, Michael. He used to be a policeman, and he did some research. He found out that you were the best man in the city for this kind of thing."

"I'm flattered."

"From what I've seen of you so far, Mr. Auster, I'm sure we've found the right man."

Quinn took this as his cue to rise. It came as a relief to stretch his legs at last. Things had gone well, far better than he had expected, but his head hurt now, and his body ached with an exhaustion he had not felt in years. If he carried on any longer, he was sure to give himself away.

"My fee is one hundred dollars a day plus expenses," he said. "If you could give me something in advance, it would be proof that I'm working for you—which would ensure us a privileged investigator-client relationship. That means everything that passes between us would be in strictest confidence."

Virginia Stillman smiled, as if at some secret joke of her own. Or perhaps she was merely responding to the possible double meaning of his last sentence. Like so many of the things that happened to him over the days and weeks that followed, Quinn could not be sure of any of it.

"How much would you like?" she asked.

"It doesn't matter. I'll leave that up to you."

"Five hundred?"

"That would be more than enough."

"Good. I'll go get my checkbook." Virginia Stillman stood up and smiled at Quinn again. "I'll get you a picture of Peter's father, too. I think I know just where it is."

Quinn thanked her and said he would wait. He watched

her leave the room and once again found himself imagining what she would look like without any clothes on. Was she somehow coming on to him, he wondered, or was it just his own mind trying to sabotage him again? He decided to postpone his meditations and take up the subject again later.

Virginia Stillman walked back into the room and said, "Here's the check. I hope I made it out correctly."

Yes, yes, thought Quinn as he examined the check, everything is tip-top. He was pleased with his own cleverness. The check, of course, was made out to Paul Auster, which meant that Quinn could not be held accountable for impersonating a private detective without a license. It reassured him to know that he had somehow put himself in the clear. The fact that he would never be able to cash the check did not trouble him. He understood, even then, that he was not doing any of this for money. He slipped the check into the inside breast pocket of his jacket.

"I'm sorry there's not a more recent photograph," Virginia Stillman was saying. "This one dates from more than twenty years ago. But I'm afraid it's the best I can do."

Quinn looked at the picture of Stillman's face, hoping for a sudden epiphany, some sudden rush of subterranean knowledge that would help him to understand the man. But the picture told him nothing. It was no more than a picture of a man. He studied it for a moment longer and concluded that it could just as easily have been anyone.

"I'll look at it more carefully when I get home," he said, putting it into the same pocket where the check had gone. "Taking the passage of time into account, I'm sure I'll be able to recognize him at the station tomorrow."

"I hope so," said Virginia Stillman. "It's terribly important, and I'm counting on you."

"Don't worry," said Quinn. "I haven't let anyone down yet."

She walked him to the door. For several seconds they stood there in silence, not knowing whether there was something to add or if the time had come to say good-bye. In that tiny interval, Virginia Stillman suddenly threw her arms around Quinn, sought out his lips with her own, and kissed him passionately, driving her tongue deep inside his mouth. Quinn was so taken off guard that he almost failed to enjoy it.

When he was at last able to breathe again, Mrs. Stillman held him at arm's length and said, "That was to prove that Peter wasn't telling you the truth. It's very important that you believe me."

"I believe you," said Quinn. "And even if I didn't believe you, it wouldn't really matter."

"I just wanted you to know what I'm capable of."

"I think I have a good idea."

She took his right hand in her two hands and kissed it. "Thank you, Mr. Auster. I really do think you're the answer."

He promised he would call her the next night, and then he found himself walking out the door, taking the elevator downstairs, and leaving the building. It was past midnight when he hit the street.

4

Q UINN had heard of cases like Peter Stillman before. Back in the days of his other life, not long after his own son was born, he had written a review of a book about the wild boy of Aveyron, and at the time he had done some research on the subject. As far as he could remember, the earliest account of such an experiment appeared in the writings of Herodotus: the Egyptian pharaoh Psamtik isolated two infants in the seventh century B.C. and commanded the servant in charge of them never to utter a word in their presence. According to Herodotus, a notoriously unreliable chronicler, the children learned to speak—their first word being the Phrygian word for bread. In the Middle Ages, the Holy Roman Emperor Frederick II repeated the experiment, hoping to discover man's true "natural language" using similar methods, but the children died before they ever spoke any words. Finally, in what was undoubtedly a hoax, the early-sixteenth-century King of Scotland, James IV, claimed that Scottish children isolated in the same manner wound up speaking "very good Hebrew."

Cranks and ideologues, however, were not the only ones

interested in the subject. Even so sane and skeptical a man as Montaigne considered the question carefully, and in his most important essay, the *Apology for Raymond Sebond*, he wrote: "I believe that a child who had been brought up in complete solitude, remote from all association (which would be a hard experiment to make), would have some sort of speech to express his ideas. And it is not credible that Nature has denied us this resource that she has given to many other animals. . . . But it is yet to be known what language this child would speak; and what has been said about it by conjecture has not much appearance of truth."

Beyond the cases of such experiments, there were also the cases of accidental isolation—children lost in the woods, sailors marooned on islands, children brought up by wolves—as well as the cases of cruel and sadistic parents who locked up their children, chained them to beds, beat them in closets, tortured them for no other reason than the compulsions of their own madness—and Quinn had read through the extensive literature devoted to these stories. There was the Scottish sailor Alexander Selkirk (thought by some to be the model for Robinson Crusoe) who had lived for four years alone on an island off the coast of Chile and who, according to the ship captain who rescued him in 1708, "had so much forgot his language for want of use, that we could scarce understand him." Less than twenty years later, Peter of Hanover, a wild child of about fourteen, who had been discovered mute and naked in a forest outside the German town of Hamelin, was brought to the English court under the special protection of George I. Both Swift and Defoe were given a chance to see him, and the experience led to Defoe's 1726 pamphlet, *Mere Nature Delineated*. Peter never learned to speak, however, and several months later was sent to the country, where he lived to the age of seventy, with no interest in sex, money, or other worldly matters. Then there was the case of Victor, the wild boy of Aveyron, who was found in 1800. Under the patient and meticulous care of Dr. Itard, Victor learned some of the rudiments of speech, but he never progressed beyond the level of a small child. Even better known than Victor was Kaspar Hauser, who appeared one afternoon in Nuremberg in 1828, dressed in an outlandish costume and barely able to utter an intelligible sound. He was able to write his name, but in all other respects he behaved like an infant. Adopted by the town and entrusted to the care of a local teacher, he spent his days sitting on the floor playing with toy horses, eating only bread and water. Kaspar nevertheless developed. He became an excellent horseman, became obsessively neat, had a passion for the colors red and white, and by all accounts displayed an extraordinary memory, especially for names and faces. Still, he preferred to remain indoors, shunned bright light, and, like Peter of Hanover, never showed any interest in sex or money. As the memory of his past gradually came back to him, he was able to recall how he had spent many years on the floor of a darkened room, fed by a man who never spoke to him or let himself be seen. Not long after these disclosures, Kasper was murdered by an unknown man with a dagger in a public park.

It had been years now since Quinn had allowed himself to think of these stories. The subject of children was too painful for him, especially children who had suffered, had been mistreated, had died before they could grow up. If Stillman was the man with the dagger, come back to avenge himself on the boy whose life he had destroyed, Quinn wanted to be there to stop him. He knew he could not bring his own son back to life, but at least he could prevent another from dying. It had suddenly become possible for him to do this, and standing there on the street now, the idea of what lay before him loomed up like a terrible dream. He thought of the little coffin that held his son's body and how he had seen it on the day of the funeral being lowered into the ground. That was isolation, he said to himself. That was silence. It did not help, perhaps, that his son's name had also been Peter.

5

A T the corner of 72nd Street and Madison Avenue, he waved down a cab. As the car rattled through the park toward the West Side, Quinn looked out the window and wondered if these were the same trees that Peter Stillman saw when he walked out into the air and the light. He wondered if Peter saw the same things he did, or whether the world was a different place for him. And if a tree was not a tree, he wondered what it really was.

After the cab had dropped him off in front of his house, Quinn realized that he was hungry. He had not eaten since breakfast early that morning. It was strange, he thought, how quickly time had passed in the Stillman apartment. If his calculations were correct, he had been there for more than fourteen hours. Within himself, however, it felt as though his stay had lasted three or four hours at most. He shrugged at the discrepancy and said to himself, "I must learn to look at my watch more often."

He retraced his path along 107th Street, turned left on Broadway, and began walking uptown, looking for a suitable place to eat. A bar did not appeal to him tonight—

eating in the dark, the press of boozy chatter—although normally he might have welcomed it. As he crossed 112th Street, he saw that the Heights Luncheonette was still open and decided to go in. It was a brightly lit yet dreary place, with a large rack of girlie magazines on one wall, an area for stationery supplies, another area for newspapers, several tables for patrons, and a long Formica counter with swivel stools. A tall Puerto Rican man in a white cardboard chef's hat stood behind the counter. It was his job to make the food, which consisted mainly of gristle-studded hamburger patties, bland sandwiches with pale tomatoes and wilted lettuce, milkshakes, egg creams, and buns. To his right, ensconced behind the cash register, was the boss, a small balding man with curly hair and a concentration camp number tattooed on his forearm, lording it over his domain of cigarettes, pipes, and cigars. He sat there impassively, reading the night-owl edition of the next morning's *Daily News*.

The place was almost deserted at that hour. At the back table sat two old men in shabby clothes, one very fat and the other very thin, intently studying the racing forms. Two empty coffee cups sat on the table between them. In the foreground, facing the magazine rack, a young student stood with an open magazine in his hands, staring at a picture of a naked woman. Quinn sat down at the counter and ordered a hamburger and a coffee. As the counterman swung into action, he spoke over his shoulder to Quinn.

"Did you see game tonight, man?"

"I missed it. Anything good to report?"

"What do you think?"

For several years Quinn had been having the same conversation with this man, whose name he did not know. Once, when he had been in the luncheonette, they had talked about baseball, and now, each time Quinn came in, they continued to talk about it. In the winter, the talk was of trades, predictions, memories. During the season, it was always the most recent game. They were both Mets fans, and the hopelessness of that passion had created a bond between them.

The counterman shook his head. "First two times up, Kingman hits solo shots," he said. "Boom, boom. Big mothers—all the way to the moon. Jones is pitching good for once and things don't look too bad. It's two to one, bottom of the ninth. Pittsburgh gets men on second and third, one out, so the Mets go to the bullpen for Allen. He walks the next guy to load them up. The Mets bring the corners in for a force at home, or maybe they can get the double play if it's hit up the middle. Peña comes up and chicken-shits a little grounder to first and the fucker goes through Kingman's legs. Two men score, and that's it, bye-bye New York."

"Dave Kingman is a turd," said Quinn, biting into his hamburger.

"But watch out for Foster," said the counterman.

"Foster's washed up. A has-been. A mean-faced bozo." Quinn chewed his food carefully, feeling with his tongue for stray bits of bone. "They should ship him back to Cincinnati by express mail."

"Yeah," said the counterman. "But they'll be tough. Better than last year, anyway."

"I don't know," said Quinn, taking another bite. "It looks good on paper, but what do they really have? Stearns is always getting hurt. They have minor leaguers at second and short, and Brooks can't keep his mind on the game. Mookie's good, but he's raw, and they can't even decide who to put in right. There's still Rusty, of course, but he's too fat to run anymore. And as for the pitching, forget it. You and I could go over to Shea tomorrow and get hired as the top two starters."

"Maybe I make you the manager," said the counterman. "You could tell those fuckers where to get off."

"You bet your bottom dollar," said Quinn.

After he finished eating, Quinn wandered over to the stationery shelves. A shipment of new notebooks had come in, and the pile was impressive, a beautiful array of blues and greens and reds and yellows. He picked one up and saw that the pages had the narrow lines he preferred. Quinn did all his writing with a pen, using a typewriter only for final drafts, and he was always on the lookout for good spiral notebooks. Now that he had embarked on the Stillman case, he felt that a new notebook was in order. It would be helpful to have a separate place to record his thoughts, his observations, and his questions. In that way, perhaps, things might not get out of control.

He looked through the pile, trying to decide which one to pick. For reasons that were never made clear to him, he suddenly felt an irresistible urge for a particular red notebook at the bottom. He pulled it out and examined it, gingerly fanning the pages with his thumb. He was at a loss to explain to himself why he found it so appealing. It was a standard eight-and-a-half-by-eleven notebook with one hundred pages. But something about it seemed to call out to him—as if its unique destiny in the world was to hold the words that came from his pen. Almost embarrassed by the intensity of his feelings, Quinn tucked the red notebook under his arm, walked over to the cash register, and bought it.

Back in his apartment a quarter of an hour later, Quinn removed the photograph of Stillman and the check from his jacket pocket and placed them carefully on his desk. He cleared the debris from the surface—dead matches, cigarette butts, eddies of ash, spent ink cartridges, a few coins, ticket stubs, doodles, a dirty handerchief—and put the red notebook in the center. Then he drew the shades in the room, took off all his clothes, and sat down at the desk. He had never done this before, but it somehow seemed appropriate to be naked at this moment. He sat there for twenty or thirty seconds, trying not to move, trying not to do anything but breathe. Then he opened the red notebook. He picked up his pen and wrote his initials, D.Q. (for Daniel Quinn), on the first page. It was the first time in more than five years that he had put his own name in one of his notebooks. He stopped to consider this fact for a moment but then dismissed it as irrelevant. He turned the page. For several moments he studied its blankness, wondering if he was not a bloody fool. Then he pressed his pen against the top line and made the first entry in the red notebook.

Stillman's face. Or: Stillman's face as it was twenty years ago. Impossible to know whether the face tomorrow will resemble it. It is certain, however, that this is not the face of a madman. Or is this not a legitimate statement? To my eyes, at least, it seems benign, if not downright pleasant. A hint of tenderness around the mouth even. More than likely blue eyes, with a tendency to water. Thin hair even then, so perhaps gone now, and what remains gray, or even white. He bears an odd familiarity: the meditative type, no doubt high-strung, someone who might stutter, fight with himself to stem the flood of words rushing from his mouth.

Little Peter. Is it necessary for me to imagine it, or can I accept it on faith? The darkness. To think of myself in that room, screaming. I am reluctant. Nor do I think I even want to understand it. To what end? This is not a story, after all. It is a fact, something happening in the world, and I am supposed to do a job, one little thing, and I have said yes to it. If all goes well, it should even be quite simple. I have not been hired to understand—merely to act. This is something new. To keep it in mind, at all costs.

And yet, what is it that Dupin says in Poe? "An identification of the reasoner's intellect with that of his opponent." But here it would apply to Stillman senior. Which is probably even worse.

As for Virginia, I am in a quandary. Not just the kiss, which might be explained by any number of reasons; not what Peter said about her, which is unimportant. Her marriage? Perhaps. The complete incongruity of it. Could it be that she's in it for the money? Or somehow working in collaboration with Stillman? That would change everything. But, at the same time, it makes no sense. For why would she have hired me? To have a witness to her apparent good intentions? Perhaps. But that seems too complicated. And yet: why do I feel she is not to be trusted?

Stillman's face, again. Thinking for these past few minutes that I have seen it before. Perhaps years ago in the neighborhood—before the time of his arrest.

To remember what it feels like to wear other people's clothes. To begin with that, I think. Assuming I must. Back in the old days, eighteen, twenty years ago, when I had no money and friends would give me things to wear. J.'s old overcoat in college, for example. And the strange sense I would have of climbing into his skin. That is probably a start.

And then, most important of all: to remember who I am. To remember who I am supposed to be. I do not think this is a game. On the other hand, nothing is clear. For example: who are you? And if you think you know, why do you keep lying about it? I have no answer. All I can say is this: listen to me. My name is Paul Auster. That is not my real name.

———————————

6

QUINN spent the next morning at the Columbia library with Stillman's book. He arrived early, the first one there as the doors opened, and the silence of the marble halls comforted him, as though he had been allowed to enter some crypt of oblivion. After flashing his alumni card at the drowsing attendant behind the desk, he retrieved the book from the stacks, returned to the third floor, and then settled down in a green leather armchair in one of the smoking rooms. The bright May morning lurked outside like a temptation, a call to wander aimlessly in the air, but Quinn fought it off. He turned the chair around, positioning himself with his back to the window, and opened the book.

The Garden and the Tower: Early Visions of the New World was divided into two parts of approximately equal length, "The Myth of Paradise" and "The Myth of Babel." The first concentrated on the discoveries of the explorers, beginning with Columbus and continuing on through Raleigh. It was Stillman's contention that the first men to visit America believed they had accidentally found paradise, a second Garden of Eden. In the narrative of his third voyage, for example, Columbus wrote: "For I believe that the earthly Paradise lies here, which no one can enter except by God's leave." As for the people of this land, Peter Martyr would write as early as 1505: "They seem to live in that golden world of which old writers speak so much, wherein men lived simply and innocently, without enforcement of laws, without quarrelling, judges, or libels, content only to satisfy nature." Or, as the ever-present Montaigne would write more than half a century later: "In my opinion, what we actually see in these nations not only surpasses all the pictures which the poets have drawn of the Golden Age, and all their inventions representing the then happy state of mankind, but also the conception and desire of philosophy itself." From the very beginning, according to Stillman, the discovery of the New World was the quickening impulse of utopian thought, the spark that gave hope to the perfectibility of human life—from Thomas More's book of 1516 to Gerónimo de Mendieta's prophecy, some years later, that America would become an ideal theocratic state, a veritable City of God.

There was, however, an opposite point of view. If some saw the Indians as living in prelapsarian innocence, there were others who judged them to be savage beasts, devils in the form of men. The discovery of cannibals in the Caribbean did nothing to assuage this opinion. The Spaniards used it as a justification to exploit the natives mercilessly for their own mercantile ends. For if you do not consider the man before you to be human, there are few restraints of conscience on your behavior towards him. It was not until 1537, with the papal bull of Paul III, that the Indians were declared to be true men possessing souls. The debate nevertheless went on for several hundred years, culminating on the one hand in the "noble savage" of Locke and Rousseau—which laid the theoretical foundations of democracy in an independent America—and, on the other hand, in the campaign to exterminate the Indians, in the undying belief that the only good Indian was a dead Indian.

The second part of the book began with a new examination of the fall. Relying heavily on Milton and his account in *Paradise Lost*—as representing the orthodox Puritan position—Stillman claimed that it was only after the fall that human life as we know it came into being. For if there was no evil in the Garden, neither was there any good. As Milton himself put it in the *Areopagitica*, "It was out of the rind of one apple tasted that good and evil leapt forth into the world, like two twins cleaving together." Stillman's gloss on this sentence was exceedingly thorough. Alert to the possibility of puns and wordplay throughout, he showed how the word "taste" was actually a reference to the Latin word "sapere," which means both "to taste" and "to know" and therefore contains a subliminal reference to the tree of knowledge: the source of the apple whose taste brought forth knowledge into the world, which is to say, good and evil. Stillman also dwelled on the paradox of the word "cleave," which means both "to join together" and "to break apart," thus embodying two equal and opposite significations, which in turn embodies a view of language that Stillman found to be present in all of Milton's work. In *Paradise Lost*, for example, each key word has two meanings—one before the fall and one after the fall. To illustrate his point, Stillman isolated several of those words—sinister, serpentine, delicious—and showed how their prelapsarian use was free of moral connotations, whereas their use after the fall was shaded, ambiguous, informed by a knowledge of evil. Adam's one task in the Garden had been to invent language, to give each creature and thing its name. In that state of innocence, his tongue had gone straight to the quick of the world. His words had not been merely appended to the things he saw, they had revealed their essences, had literally brought them to life. A thing and its name were interchangeable. After the fall, this was no longer true. Names became detached from things; words devolved into a collection of arbitrary signs; language had been severed from God. The story of the Garden, therefore, records not only the fall of man, but the fall of language.

Later in the Book of Genesis there is another story about language. According to Stillman, the Tower of Babel episode was an exact recapitulation of what happened in the Garden—only expanded, made general in its significance for all mankind. The story takes on special meaning when its placement in the book is considered: chapter eleven of Genesis, verses one through nine. This is the very last incident of prehistory in the Bible. After that, the Old Testament is exclusively a chronicle of the Hebrews. In other words, the Tower of Babel stands as the last image before the true beginning of the world.

Stillman's commentaries went on for many pages. He began with a historical survey of the various exegetical traditions concerning the story, elaborated on the numerous misreadings that had grown up around it, and ended with a lengthy catalogue of legends from the Haggadah (a compendium of rabbinical interpretations not connected with legal matters). It was generally accepted, wrote Stillman, that the Tower had been built in the year 1996 after the creation, a scant 340 years after the Flood, "lest we be scattered abroad upon the face of the whole earth." God's punishment came as a response to this desire, which contradicted a command that had appeared earlier in Genesis: "Be fertile and increase, fill the earth and master it." By destroying the Tower, therefore, God condemned man to obey this injunction. Another reading, however, saw the Tower as a challenge against God. Nimrod, the first ruler of all the world, was designated as the Tower's architect: Babel was to be a shrine that symbolized the universality of his power. This was the Promethean view of the story, and it hinged on the phrases "whose top may reach unto heaven" and "let us make a name." The building of the

Tower became the obsessive, overriding passion of mankind, more important finally than life itself. Bricks became more precious than people. Women laborers did not even stop to give birth to their children; they secured the newborn in their aprons and went right on working. Apparently, there were three different groups involved in the construction: those who wanted to dwell in heaven, those who wanted to wage war against God, and those who wanted to worship idols. At the same time, they were united in their efforts—"And the whole earth was of one language, and of one speech"—and the latent power of a united mankind outraged God. "And the Lord said, Behold, the people is one, and they have all one language; and this they begin to do: and now nothing will be restrained from them, which they have imagined to do." This speech is a conscious echo of the words God spoke on expelling Adam and Eve from the Garden: "Behold, the man is become one of us, to know good and evil; and now, lest he put forth his hand, and take also of the tree of life, and eat, and live forever—Therefore the Lord God sent him forth from the garden of Eden. . . ." Still another reading held that the story was intended merely as a way of explaining the diversity of peoples and languages. For if all men were descended from Noah and his sons, how was it possible to account for the vast differences among cultures? Another, similar reading contended that the story was an explanation of the existence of paganism and idolatry—for until this story all men are presented as being monotheistic in their beliefs. As for the Tower itself, legend had it that one third of the structure sank into the ground, one third was destroyed by fire, and one third was left standing. God attacked it in two ways in order to convince man that the destruction was a divine punishment and not the result of chance. Still, the part left standing was so high that a palm tree seen from the top of it appeared no larger than a grasshopper. It was also said that a person could walk for three days in the shadow of the Tower without ever leaving it. Finally—and Stillman dwelled upon this at great length—whoever looked upon the ruins of the Tower was believed to forget everything he knew.

What all this had to do with the New World Quinn could not say. But then a new chapter started, and suddenly Stillman was discussing the life of Henry Dark, a Boston clergyman who was born in London in 1649 (on the day of Charles I's execution), came to America in 1675, and died in a fire in Cambridge, Massachusetts, in 1691.

According to Stillman, as a young man Henry Dark had served as private secretary to John Milton—from 1669 until the poet's death five years later. This was news to Quinn, for he seemed to remember reading somewhere that the blind Milton had dictated his work to one of his daughters. Dark, he learned, was an ardent Puritan, a student of theology, and a devoted follower of Milton's work. Having met his hero one evening at a small gathering, he was invited to pay a call the following week. That led to further calls, until eventually Milton began to entrust Dark with various small tasks: taking dictation, guiding him through the streets of London, reading to him from the works of the ancients. In a 1672 letter written by Dark to his sister in Boston, he mentioned long discussions with Milton on the finer points of Biblical exegesis. Then Milton died, and Dark was disconsolate. Six months later, finding England a desert, a land that offered him nothing, he decided to emigrate to America. He arrived in Boston in the summer of 1675.

Little was known of his first years in the New World. Stillman speculated that he might have travelled westward, foraging out into unchartered territory, but no concrete evidence could be found to support this view. On the other hand, certain references in Dark's writings indicated an intimate knowledge of Indian customs, which led Stillman to theorize that Dark might possibly have lived among one of the tribes for a period of time. Be that as it may, there was no public mention of Dark until 1682, when his name was entered in the Boston marriage registry as having taken one Lucy Fitts as his bride. Two years later, he was listed as heading a small Puritan congregation on the outskirts of the city. Several children were born to the couple, but all of them died in infancy. A son John, however, born in 1686, survived. But in 1691 the boy was reported to have fallen accidentally from a second-story window and perished. Just one month later, the entire house went up in flames, and both Dark and his wife were killed.

Henry Dark would have passed into the obscurity of early American life if not for one thing: the publication of a pamphlet in 1690 entitled *The New Babel*. According to Stillman, this little work of sixty-four pages was the most visionary account of the new continent that had been written up to that time. If Dark had not died so soon after its appearance, its effect would no doubt have been greater. For, as it turned out, most of the copies of the pamphlet were destroyed in the fire that killed Dark. Stillman himself had been able to discover only one—and that by accident, in the attic of his family's house in Cambridge. After years of diligent research, he had concluded that this was the only copy still in existence.

The New Babel, written in bold, Miltonic prose, presented the case for the building of paradise in America. Unlike the other writers on the subject, Dark did not assume paradise to be a place that could be discovered. There were no maps that could lead a man to it, no instruments of navigation that could guide a man to its shores. Rather, its existence was immanent within man himself: the idea of a beyond he might someday create in the here and now. For utopia was nowhere—even, as Dark explained, in its "wordhood." And if man could bring forth this dreamed-of place, it would only be by building it with his own two hands.

Dark based his conclusions on a reading of the Babel story as a prophetic work. Drawing heavily on Milton's interpretation of the fall, he followed his master in placing an inordinate importance on the role of language. But he took the poet's ideas one step further. If the fall of man also entailed a fall of language, was it not logical to assume that it would be possible to undo the fall, to reverse its effects by undoing the fall of language, by striving to re-create the language that was spoken in Eden? If man could learn to speak this original language of innocence, did it not follow that he would thereby recover a state of inno-cence within himself? We had only to look at the example of Christ, Dark argued, to understand that this was so. For was Christ not a man, a creature of flesh and blood? And did not Christ speak this prelapsarian language? In Mil-ton's *Paradise Regained*, Satan speaks with "double-sense deluding," whereas Christ's "actions to his words accord, his words / To his large heart give utterance due, his heart / Contains of good, wise, just, the perfect shape." And had God not "now sent his living Oracle / Into the World to teach his final will, / And sends his Spirit of Truth henceforth to dwell / In pious Hearts, an inward Oracle / To all Truth requisite for me to know"? And, because of Christ, did the fall not have a happy outcome, was it not a *felix culpa*, as doctrine instructs? Therefore, Dark con-tended, it would indeed be possible for man to speak the original language of innocence and to recover, whole and unbroken, the truth within himself.

Turning to the Babel story, Dark then elaborated his plan and announced his vision of things to come. Quoting from the second verse of Genesis 11—"And it came to pass, as they journeyed from the east, that they found a plain in the land of Shi-nar; and they dwelt there"—Dark stated that this passage proved the westward movement of human life and civilization. For the city of Babel—or Babylon—was situated in Mesopotamia, far east of the land of the Hebrews. If Babel lay to the west of anything, it was Eden, the original site of mankind. Man's duty to scatter himself across the whole earth—in response to God's command to "be fertile . . . and fill the earth"— would inevitably move along a western course. And what more western land in all Christendom, Dark asked, than America? The movement of English settlers to the New World, therefore, could be read as the fulfillment of the ancient commandment. America was the last step in the process. Once the continent had been filled, the moment would be ripe for a change in the fortunes of mankind. The impediment to the building of Babel—that man must fill the earth—would be eliminated. At that moment it would again be possible for the whole earth to be of one language and one speech. And if that were to happen, paradise could not be far behind.

Just as Babel had been built 340 years after the Flood, so it would be, Dark predicted, exactly 340 years after the arrival of the *Mayflower* at Plymouth that the commandment would be carried out. For surely it was the Puritans, God's newly chosen people, who held the destiny of mankind in their hands. Unlike the Hebrews, who had failed God by refusing to accept his son, these transplanted Englishmen would write the final chapter of history before heaven and earth were joined at last. Like Noah in his ark, they had traveled across the vast oceanic flood to carry out their holy mission.

Three hundred and forty years, according to Dark's calculations, meant that in 1960 the first part of the settlers' work would have been done. At that point, the foundations would have been laid for the real work that was to follow: the building of the new Babel. Already, Dark wrote, he saw encouraging signs in the city of Boston, for there, as nowhere else in the world, the chief construction material was brick—which, as set forth in verse three of Genesis 11, was specified as the construction material of Babel. In the year 1960, he stated confidently, the new Babel would begin to go up, its very shape aspiring toward the heavens, a symbol of the resurrection of the human spirit. History would be written in reverse. What had fallen would be raised up; what had been broken would be made whole. Once completed, the Tower would be large enough to hold every inhabitant of the New World. There would be a room for each person, and once he entered that room, he would forget everything he knew. After forty days and forty nights, he would emerge a new man, speaking God's language, prepared to inhabit the second, everlasting paradise.

So ended Stillman's synopsis of Henry Dark's pamphlet, dated December 26, 1690, the seventieth anniversary of the landing of the *Mayflower*.

Quinn let out a little sigh and closed the book. The reading room was empty. He leaned forward, put his head in his hands, and closed his eyes. "Nineteen sixty," he said aloud. He tried to conjure up an image of Henry Dark, but nothing came to him. In his mind he saw only fire, a blaze of burning books. Then, losing track of his thoughts and where they had been leading him, he suddenly remembered that 1960 was the year that Stillman had locked up his son.

He opened the red notebook and set it squarely on his lap. Just as he was about to write in it, however, he decided that he had had enough. He closed the red notebook, got up from his chair, and returned Stillman's book to the front desk. Lighting a cigarette at the bottom of the stairs, he left the library and walked out into the May afternoon.

7

H E made it to Grand Central well in advance. Stillman's train was not due to arrive until six-forty-one, but Quinn wanted time to study the geography of the place, to make sure that Stillman would not be able to slip away from him. As he emerged from the subway and entered the great hall, he saw by the clock that it was just past four. Already the station had begun to fill with the rush-hour crowd. Making his way through the press of oncoming bodies, Quinn made a tour of the numbered gates, looking for hidden staircases, unmarked exits, dark alcoves. He concluded that a man determined to disappear could do so without much trouble. He would have to hope that Stillman had not been warned that he would be there. If that were the case, and Stillman managed to elude him, it would mean that Virginia Stillman was responsible. There was no one else. It solaced him to know that he had an alternate plan if things went awry. If Stillman did not show up, Quinn would go straight to 69th Street and confront Virginia Stillman with what he knew.

As he wandered through the station, he reminded him-

self of who he was supposed to be. The effect of being
Paul Auster, he had begun to learn, was not altogether
unpleasant. Although he still had the same body, the same
mind, the same thoughts, he felt as though he had somehow
been taken out of himself, as if he no longer had to walk
around with the burden of his own consciousness. By a
simple trick of the intelligence, a deft little twist of naming,
he felt incomparably lighter and freer. At the same time,
he knew it was all an illusion. But there was a certain
comfort in that. He had not really lost himself; he was
merely pretending, and he could return to being Quinn
whenever he wished. The fact that there was now a purpose
to his being Paul Auster—a purpose that was becoming
more and more important to him—served as a kind of
moral justification for the charade and absolved him of
having to defend his lie. For imagining himself as Auster
had become synonymous in his mind with doing good in
the world.

He wandered through the station, then, as if inside the
body of Paul Auster, waiting for Stillman to appear. He
looked up at the vaulted ceiling of the great hall and studied
the fresco of constellations. There were light bulbs representing the stars and line drawings of the celestial figures. Quinn had never been able to grasp the connection
between the constellations and their names. As a boy he
had spent many hours under the night sky trying to tally

the clusters of pinprick lights with the shapes of bears, bulls, archers, and water carriers. But nothing had ever come of it, and he had felt stupid, as though there were a blind spot in the center of his brain. He wondered if the young Auster had been any better at it than he was.

Across the way, occupying the greater part of the station's east wall, was the Kodak display photograph, with its bright, unearthly colors. The scene that month showed a street in some New England fishing village, perhaps Nantucket. A beautiful spring light shone on the cobblestones, flowers of many colors stood in window boxes along the house fronts, and far down at the end of the street was the ocean, with its white waves and blue, blue water. Quinn remembered visiting Nantucket with his wife long ago, in her first month of pregnancy, when his son was no more than a tiny almond in her belly. He found it painful to think of that now, and he tried to suppress the pictures that were forming in his head. "Look at it through Auster's eyes," he said to himself, "and don't think of anything else." He turned his attention to the photograph again and was relieved to find his thoughts wandering to the subject of whales, to the expeditions that had set out from Nantucket in the last century, to Melville and the opening pages of *Moby Dick*. From there his mind drifted off to the accounts he had read of Melville's last years—the taciturn old man working in the New York customs house, with no readers, forgotten by everyone. Then, suddenly, with great clarity and precision, he saw Bartleby's window and the blank brick wall before him.

Someone tapped him on the arm, and as Quinn wheeled to meet the assault, he saw a short, silent man holding out a green and red ballpoint pen to him. Stapled to the pen was a little white paper flag, one side of which read: "This good article is the Courtesy of a DEAF MUTE. Pay any price. Thank you for your help." On the other side of the flag there was a chart of the manual alphabet—LEARN TO SPEAK TO YOUR FRIENDS—that showed the hand positions for each of the twenty-six letters. Quinn reached into his pocket and gave the man a dollar. The deaf mute nodded once very briefly and then moved on, leaving Quinn with the pen in his hand.

It was now past five o'clock. Quinn decided he would be less vulnerable in another spot and removed himself to the waiting room. This was generally a grim place, filled with dust and people with nowhere to go, but now, with the rush hour at full force, it had been taken over by men and women with briefcases, books, and newspapers. Quinn had trouble finding a seat. After searching for two or three minutes, he finally found a place on one of the benches, wedging himself between a man in a blue suit and a plump young woman. The man was reading the sports section of the *Times*, and Quinn glanced over to read the account of the Mets' loss the night before. He had made it to the third or fourth paragraph when the man turned slowly toward him, gave him a vicious stare, and jerked the paper out of view.

After that, a strange thing happened. Quinn turned his attention to the young woman on his right, to see if there was any reading material in that direction. Quinn guessed her age at around twenty. There were several pimples on her left cheek, obscured by a pinkish smear of pancake makeup, and a wad of chewing gum was crackling in her mouth. She was, however, reading a book, a paperback with a lurid cover, and Quinn leaned ever so slightly to his right to catch a glimpse of the title. Against all his expectations, it was a book he himself had written—*Suicide Squeeze* by William Wilson, the first of the Max Work novels. Quinn had often imagined this situation: the sudden, unexpected pleasure of encountering one of his readers. He had even imagined the conversation that would follow: he, suavely diffident as the stranger praised the book, and then, with great reluctance and modesty, agreeing to autograph the title page, "since you insist." But now that the scene was taking place, he felt quite disappointed, even angry. He did not like the girl sitting next to him, and it offended him that she should be casually skimming the pages that had cost him so much effort. His impulse was to tear the book out of her hands and run across the station with it.

He looked at her face again, trying to hear the words

she was sounding out in her head, watching her eyes as they darted back and forth across the page. He must have been looking too hard, for a moment later she turned to him with an irritated expression on her face and said, "You got a problem, mister?"

Quinn smiled weakly. "No problem," he said. "I was just wondering if you liked the book."

The girl shrugged. "I've read better and I've read worse."

Quinn wanted to drop the conversation right there, but something in him persisted. Before he could get up and leave, the words were already out of his mouth. "Do you find it exciting?"

The girl shrugged again and cracked her gum loudly. "Sort of. There's a part where the detective gets lost that's kind of scary."

"Is he a smart detective?"

"Yeah, he's smart. But he talks too much."

"You'd like more action?"

"I guess so."

"If you don't like it, why do you go on reading?"

"I don't know." The girl shrugged once again. "It passes the time, I guess. Anyway, it's no big deal. It's just a book."

He was about to tell her who he was, but then he realized that it made no difference. The girl was beyond hope. For five years he had kept William Wilson's identity a secret, and he wasn't about to give it away now, least of all to an imbecile stranger. Still, it was painful, and he struggled desperately to swallow his pride. Rather than punch the girl in the face, he abruptly stood up from his seat and walked away.

At six-thirty he posted himself in front of gate twenty-four. The train was due to arrive on time, and from his vantage in the center of the doorway, Quinn judged that his chances of seeing Stillman were good. He took out the photograph from his pocket and studied it again, paying special attention to the eyes. He remembered having read somewhere that the eyes were the one feature of the face that never changed. From childhood to old age they remained the same, and a man with the head to see it could theoretically look into the eyes of a boy in a photograph and recognize the same person as an old man. Quinn had his doubts, but this was all he had to go on, his only bridge to the present. Once again, however, Stillman's face told him nothing.

The train pulled into the station, and Quinn felt the noise of it shoot through his body: a random, hectic din that seemed to join with his pulse, pumping his blood in raucous spurts. His head then filled with Peter Stillman's voice, as a barrage of nonsense words clattered against the walls of his skull. He told himself to stay calm. But that did little good. In spite of what he had been expecting of himself at this moment, he was excited.

The train was crowded, and as the passengers started filling the ramp and walking toward him, they quickly became a mob. Quinn flapped the red notebook nervously against his right thigh, stood on his tiptoes, and peered into the throng. Soon the people were surging around him. There were men and women, children and old people, teenagers and babies, rich people and poor people, black men and white women, white men and black women, Orientals and Arabs, men in brown and gray and blue and green, women in red and white and yellow and pink, children in sneakers, children in shoes, children in cowboy boots, fat people and thin people, tall people and short people, each one different from all the others, each one irreducibly himself. Quinn watched them all, anchored to his spot, as if his whole being had been exiled to his eyes. Each time an elderly man approached, he braced himself for it to be Stillman. They came and went too quickly for him to indulge in disappointment, but in each old face he seemed to find an augur of what the real Stillman would be like, and he rapidly shifted his expectations with each new face, as if the accumulation of old men was heralding the imminent arrival of Stillman himself. For one brief instant Quinn thought, "So this is what detective work is like." But other than that he thought nothing. He watched. Immobile among the moving crowd, he stood there and watched.

With about half the passengers now gone, Quinn had

his first sight of Stillman. The resemblance to the photograph seemed unmistakable. No, he had not gone bald, as Quinn had thought he would. His hair was white, and it lay on his head uncombed, sticking up here and there in tufts. He was tall, thin, without question past sixty, somewhat stooped. Inappropriately for the season, he wore a long brown overcoat that had gone to seed, and he shuffled slightly as he walked. The expression on his face seemed placid, midway between a daze and thoughtfulness. He did not look at the things around him, nor did they seem to interest him. He had one piece of luggage, a once beautiful but now battered leather suitcase with a strap around it. Once or twice as he walked up the ramp he put the suitcase down and rested for a moment. He seemed to be moving with effort, a bit thrown by the crowd, uncertain whether to keep up with it or to let the others pass him by.

Quinn backed off several feet, positioning himself for a quick move to the left or right, depending on what happened. At the same time, he wanted to be far enough away so that Stillman would not feel he was being followed.

As Stillman reached the threshold of the station, he put his bag down once again and paused. At that moment Quinn allowed himself a glance to Stillman's right, surveying the rest of the crowd to be doubly sure he had made no mistakes. What happened then defied explanation. Directly behind Stillman, heaving into view just inches behind his right shoulder, another man stopped, took a lighter out of his pocket, and lit a cigarette. His face was the exact twin of Stillman's. For a second Quinn thought it was an illusion, a kind of aura thrown off by the electromagnetic currents in Stillman's body. But no, this other Stillman moved, breathed, blinked his eyes; his actions were clearly independent of the first Stillman. The second Stillman had a prosperous air about him. He was dressed in an expensive blue suit; his shoes were shined; his white hair was combed; and in his eyes there was the shrewd look of a man of the world. He, too, was carrying a single bag: an elegant black suitcase, about the same size as the other Stillman's.

Quinn froze. There was nothing he could do now that would not be a mistake. Whatever choice he made—and he had to make a choice—would be arbitrary, a submission to chance. Uncertainty would haunt him to the end. At that moment, the two Stillmans started on their way again. The first turned right, the second turned left. Quinn craved an amoeba's body, wanting to cut himself in half and run off in two directions at once. "Do something," he said to himself, "do something now, you idiot."

For no reason, he went to his left, in pursuit of the second Stillman. After nine or ten paces, he stopped. Something told him he would live to regret what he was doing. He was acting out of spite, spurred on to punish the second Stillman for confusing him. He turned around and saw the first Stillman shuffling off in the other direction. Surely this was his man. This shabby creature, so broken down and disconnected from his surroundings— surely this was the mad Stillman. Quinn breathed deeply, exhaled with a trembling chest, and breathed in again. There was no way to know: not this, not anything. He went after the first Stillman, slowing his pace to match the old man's, and followed him to the subway.

It was nearly seven o'clock now, and the crowds had begun to thin out. Although Stillman seemed to be in a fog, he nevertheless knew where he was going. The professor went straight for the subway staircase, paid his money at the token booth below, and waited calmly on the platform for the Times Square Shuttle. Quinn began to lose his fear of being noticed. He had never seen anyone so lost in his own thoughts. Even if he stood directly in front of him, he doubted that Stillman would be able to see him.

They traveled to the West Side on the shuttle, walked through the dank corridors of the 42nd Street station, and went down another set of stairs to the IRT trains. Seven or eight minutes later they boarded the Broadway express, careened uptown for two long stops, and got off at 96th Street. Slowly making their way up the final staircase, with several pauses as Stillman set down his bag and caught his breath, they surfaced on the corner and entered the indigo evening. Stillman did not hesitate. Without stopping to get his bearings, he began walking up Broadway along

the east side of the street. For several minutes Quinn toyed
with the irrational conviction that Stillman was walking
toward his house on 107th Street. But before he could
indulge himself in a full-blown panic, Stillman stopped
at the corner of 99th Street, waited for the light to change
from red to green, and crossed over to the other side of
Broadway. Halfway up the block there was a small fleabag
for down-and-outs, the Hotel Harmony. Quinn had passed
it many times before, and he was familiar with the winos
and vagabonds who hung around the place. It surprised
him to see Stillman open the front door and enter the lobby.
Somehow he had assumed the old man would have found
more comfortable lodgings. But as Quinn stood outside the
glass-paneled door and saw the professor walk up to the
desk, write what was undoubtedly his name in the guest
book, pick up his bag and disappear into the elevator, he
realized that this was where Stillman meant to stay.

Quinn waited outside for the next two hours, pacing up
and down the block, thinking that Stillman would perhaps
emerge to look for dinner in one of the local coffee shops.
But the old man did not appear, and at last Quinn decided
he must have gone to sleep. He put in a call to Virginia
Stillman from a pay booth on the corner, gave her a full
report of what had happened, and then headed home to
107th Street.

8

THE next morning, and for many mornings to follow, Quinn posted himself on a bench in the middle of the traffic island at Broadway and 99th Street. He would arrive early, never later than seven o'clock, and sit there with a take-out coffee, a buttered roll, and an open newspaper on his lap, watching the glass door of the hotel. By eight o'clock Stillman would come out, always in his long brown overcoat, carrying a large, old-fashioned carpet bag. For two weeks this routine did not vary. The old man would wander through the streets of the neighborhood, advancing slowly, sometimes by the merest of increments, pausing, moving on again, pausing once more, as though each step had to be weighed and measured before it could take its place among the sum total of steps. Moving in this manner was difficult for Quinn. He was used to walking briskly, and all this starting and stopping and shuffling began to be a strain, as though the rhythm of his body was being disrupted. He was the hare in pursuit of the tortoise, and again and again he had to remind himself to hold back.

What Stillman did on these walks remained something of a mystery to Quinn. He could, of course, see with his own eyes what happened, and all these things he dutifully recorded in his red notebook. But the meaning of these things continued to elude him. Stillman never seemed to be going anywhere in particular, nor did he seem to know where he was. And yet, as if by conscious design, he kept to a narrowly circumscribed area, bounded on the north by 110th Street, on the south by 72nd Street, on the west by Riverside Park, and on the east by Amsterdam Avenue. No matter how haphazard his journeys seemed to be—and each day his itinerary was different—Stillman never crossed these borders. Such precision baffled Quinn, for in all other respects Stillman seemed to be aimless.

As he walked, Stillman did not look up. His eyes were permanently fixed on the pavement, as though he were searching for something. Indeed, every now and then he would stoop down, pick some object off the ground, and examine it closely, turning it over and over in his hand. It made Quinn think of an archeologist inspecting a shard at some prehistoric ruin. Occasionally, after poring over an object in this way, Stillman would toss it back onto the sidewalk. But more often than not he would open his bag and lay the object gently inside it. Then, reaching into one of his coat pockets, he would remove a red notebook— similar to Quinn's but smaller—and write in it with great concentration for a minute or two. Having completed this operation, he would return the notebook to his pocket, pick up his bag, and continue on his way.

As far as Quinn could tell, the objects Stillman collected were valueless. They seemed to be no more than broken things, discarded things, stray bits of junk. Over the days that passed, Quinn noted a collapsible umbrella shorn of its material, the severed head of a rubber doll, a black glove, the bottom of a shattered light bulb, several pieces of printed matter (soggy magazines, shredded newspapers), a torn photograph, anonymous machinery parts, and sundry other clumps of flotsam he could not identify. The fact that Stillman took this scavenging seriously intrigued Quinn, but he could do no more than observe, write down what he saw in the red notebook, hover stupidly on the surface of things. At the same time, it pleased him to know that Stillman also had a red notebook, as if this formed a secret link between them. Quinn suspected that Stillman's red notebook contained answers to the questions that had been accumulating in his mind, and he began to plot various stratagems for stealing it from the old man. But the time had not yet come for such a step.

Other than picking up objects from the street, Stillman seemed to do nothing. Every now and then he would stop somewhere for a meal. Occasionally he would bump into someone and mumble an apology. Once a car nearly ran him over as he was crossing the street. Stillman did not talk to anyone, did not go into any stores, did not smile. He seemed neither happy nor sad. Twice, when his scavenging haul had been unusually large, he returned to the hotel in the middle of the day and then re-emerged a few minutes later with an empty bag. On most days he spent at least several hours in Riverside Park, walking methodically along the macadam footpaths or else thrashing through the bushes with a stick. His quest for objects did not abate amidst the greenery. Stones, leaves, and twigs all found their way into his bag. Once, Quinn observed, he even stooped down for a dried dog turd, sniffed it carefully, and kept it. It was in the park, too, that Stillman rested. In the afternoon, often following his lunch, he would sit on a bench and gaze out across the Hudson. Once, on a particularly warm day, Quinn saw him sprawled out on the grass asleep. When darkness came, Stillman would eat dinner at the Apollo Coffee Shop on 97th Street and Broadway and then return to his hotel for the night. Not once did he try to contact his son. This was confirmed by Virginia Stillman, whom Quinn called each night after returning home.

The essential thing was to stay involved. Little by little, Quinn began to feel cut off from his original intentions, and he wondered now if he had not embarked on a meaningless project. It was possible, of course, that Stillman was merely biding his time, lulling the world into lethargy before striking. But that would assume he was aware of being watched, and Quinn felt that was unlikely. He had done his job well so far, keeping at a discreet distance from the old man, blending into the traffic of the street, neither calling attention to himself nor taking drastic measures to keep himself hidden. On the other hand, it was possible that Stillman had known all along that he would be watched—had even known it in advance—and therefore had not taken the trouble to discover who the particular watcher was. If being followed was a certainty, what did it matter? A watcher, once discovered, could always be replaced by another.

This view of the situation comforted Quinn, and he decided to believe in it, even though he had no grounds for belief. Either Stillman knew what he was doing or he didn't. And if he didn't, then Quinn was going nowhere, was wasting his time. How much better it was to believe that all his steps were actually to some purpose. If this interpretation required knowledge on Stillman's part, then Quinn would accept this knowledge as an article of faith, at least for the time being.

There remained the problem of how to occupy his thoughts as he followed the old man. Quinn was used to wandering. His excursions through the city had taught him to understand the connectedness of inner and outer. Using aimless

motion as a technique of reversal, on his best days he
could bring the outside in and thus usurp the sovereignty
of inwardness. By flooding himself with externals, by
drowning himself out of himself, he had managed to exert
some small degree of control over his fits of despair. Wandering, therefore, was a kind of mindlessness. But following Stillman was not wandering. Stillman could wander,
he could stagger like a blindman from one spot to another,
but this was a privilege denied to Quinn. For he was obliged
now to concentrate on what he was doing, even if it was
next to nothing. Time and again his thoughts would begin
to drift, and soon thereafter his steps would follow suit.
This meant that he was constantly in danger of quickening
his pace and crashing into Stillman from behind. To guard
against this mishap he devised several different methods
of deceleration. The first was to tell himself that he was
no longer Daniel Quinn. He was Paul Auster now, and
with each step he took he tried to fit more comfortably into
the strictures of that transformation. Auster was no more
than a name to him, a husk without content. To be Auster
meant being a man with no interior, a man with no thoughts.
And if there were no thoughts available to him, if his own
inner life had been made inaccessible, then there was no
place for him to retreat to. As Auster he could not summon
up any memories or fears, any dreams or joys, for all these
things, as they pertained to Auster, were a blank to him.

He consequently had to remain solely on his own surface, looking outward for sustenance. To keep his eyes fixed on Stillman, therefore, was not merely a distraction from the train of his thoughts, it was the only thought he allowed himself to have.

For a day or two this tactic was mildly successful, but eventually even Auster began to droop from the monotony. Quinn realized that he needed something more to keep himself occupied, some little task to accompany him as he went about his work. In the end, it was the red notebook that offered him salvation. Instead of merely jotting down a few casual comments, as he had done the first few days, he decided to record every detail about Stillman he possibly could. Using the pen he had bought from the deaf mute, he set about his task with diligence. Not only did he take note of Stillman's gestures, describe each object he selected or rejected for his bag, and keep an accurate timetable for all events, but he also set down with meticulous care an exact itinerary of Stillman's divagations, noting each street he followed, each turn he made, and each pause that occurred. In addition to keeping him busy, the red notebook slowed Quinn's pace. There was no danger now of overtaking Stillman. The problem, rather, was to keep up with him, to make sure he did not vanish. For walking and writing were not easily compatible activities. If for the past five years Quinn had spent his days doing the one and the other, now he was trying to do them both at the same time. In the beginning he made many mistakes. It was especially difficult to write without looking at the page, and he often discovered that he had written two or even three lines on top of each other, producing a jumbled, illegible palimpsest. To look at the page, however, meant stopping, and this would increase his chances of losing Stillman. After a time, he decided that it was basically a question of position. He experimented with the notebook in front of him at a forty-five-degree angle, but he found his left wrist soon tired. After that, he tried keeping the notebook directly in front of his face, eyes peering over it like some Kilroy come to life, but this proved impractical. Next, he tried propping the notebook on his right arm several inches above his elbow and supporting the back of the notebook with his left palm. But this cramped his writing hand and made writing on the bottom half of the page impossible. Finally, he decided to rest the notebook on his left hip, much as an artist holds his palette. This was an improvement. The carrying no longer caused a strain, and his right hand could hold the pen unencumbered by other duties. Although this method also had its drawbacks, it seemed to be the most comfortable arrangement over the long haul. For Quinn was now able to divide his attention almost equally between Stillman and his writing, glancing now up at the one, now down at the other, seeing the thing and writing about it in the same fluid gesture. With the deaf mute's pen in his right hand and the red notebook on his left hip, Quinn went on following Stillman for another nine days.

His nightly conversations with Virginia Stillman were brief. Although the memory of the kiss was still sharp in Quinn's mind, there had been no further romantic developments. At first, Quinn had expected something to happen. After such a promising start, he felt certain that he would eventually find Mrs. Stillman in his arms. But his employer had rapidly retreated behind the mask of business and not once had referred to that isolated moment of passion. Perhaps Quinn had been misguided in his hopes, momentarily confusing himself with Max Work, a man who never failed to profit from such situations. Or perhaps it was simply that Quinn was beginning to feel his loneliness more keenly. It had been a long time since a warm body had been beside him. For the fact was, he had started lusting after Virginia Stillman the moment he saw her, well before the kiss took place. Nor did her current lack of encouragement prevent him from continuing to imagine her naked. Lascivious pictures marched through Quinn's head each night, and although the chances of their becoming real seemed remote, they remained a pleasant diversion. Much later, long after it was too late, he realized that deep in-

side he had been nurturing the chivalric hope of solving
the case so brilliantly, of removing Peter Stillman from
danger so swiftly and irrevocably, that he would win
Mrs. Stillman's desire for as long as he wanted it. That,
of course, was a mistake. But of all the mistakes Quinn
made from beginning to end, it was no worse than any
other.

It was the thirteenth day since the case had begun.
Quinn returned home that evening out of sorts. He was
discouraged, ready to abandon ship. In spite of the games
he had been playing with himself, in spite of the stories
he had made up to keep himself going, there seemed to
be no substance to the case. Stillman was a crazy old man
who had forgotten his son. He could be followed to the
end of time, and still nothing would happen. Quinn picked
up the phone and dialed the Stillman apartment.

"I'm about ready to pack it in," he said to Virginia
Stillman. "From all I've seen, there's no threat to Peter."

"That's just what he wants us to think," the woman
answered. "You have no idea how clever he is. And how
patient."

"He might be patient, but I'm not. I think you're wasting
your money. And I'm wasting my time."

"Are you sure he hasn't seen you? That could make all
the difference."

"I wouldn't stake my life on it, but yes, I'm sure."

"What are you saying, then?"

"I'm saying you have nothing to worry about. At least for now. If anything happens later, contact me. I'll come running at the first sign of trouble."

After a pause Virginia Stillman said, "You could be right." Then, after another pause, "But just to reassure me a little, I wonder if we could compromise."

"It depends on what you have in mind."

"Just this. Give it a few more days. To make absolutely certain."

"On one condition," said Quinn. "You've got to let me do it in my own way. No more restraints. I have to be free to talk to him, to question him, to get to the bottom of it once and for all."

"Wouldn't that be risky?"

"You don't have to worry. I'm not going to tip our hand. He won't even guess who I am or what I'm up to."

"How will you manage that?"

"That's my problem. I have all kinds of tricks up my sleeve. You just have to trust me."

"All right, I'll go along. I don't suppose it will hurt."

"Good. I'll give it a few more days, and then we'll see where we stand."

"Mr. Auster?"

"Yes?"

"I'm terribly grateful. Peter has been in such good shape

these past two weeks, and I know it's because of you. He talks about you all the time. You're like . . . I don't know . . . a hero to him."

"And how does Mrs. Stillman feel?"

"She feels much the same way."

"That's good to hear. Maybe someday she'll allow me to feel grateful to her."

"Anything is possible, Mr. Auster. You should remember that."

"I will. I'd be a fool not to."

Quinn made a light supper of scrambled eggs and toast, drank a bottle of beer, and then settled down at his desk with the red notebook. He had been writing in it now for many days, filling page after page with his erratic, jostled hand, but he had not yet had the heart to read over what he had written. Now that the end at last seemed in sight, he thought he might hazard a look.

Much of it was hard going, especially in the early parts. And when he did manage to decipher the words, it did not seem to have been worth the trouble. "Picks up pencil in middle of block. Examines, hesitates, puts in bag. . . . Buys sandwich in deli. . . . Sits on bench in park and reads through red notebook." These sentences seemed utterly worthless to him.

It was all a question of method. If the object was to

understand Stillman, to get to know him well enough to be able to anticipate what he would do next, Quinn had failed. He had started with a limited set of facts: Stillman's background and profession, the imprisonment of his son, his arrest and hospitalization, a book of bizarre scholarship written while he was supposedly still sane, and above all Virginia Stillman's certainty that he would now try to harm his son. But the facts of the past seemed to have no bearing on the facts of the present. Quinn was deeply disillusioned. He had always imagined that the key to good detective work was a close observation of details. The more accurate the scrutiny, the more successful the results. The implication was that human behavior could be understood, that beneath the infinite facade of gestures, tics, and silences, there was finally a coherence, an order, a source of motivation. But after struggling to take in all these surface effects, Quinn felt no closer to Stillman than when he first started following him. He had lived Stillman's life, walked at his pace, seen what he had seen, and the only thing he felt now was the man's impenetrability. Instead of narrowing the distance that lay between him and Stillman, he had seen the old man slip away from him, even as he remained before his eyes.

For no particular reason that he was aware of, Quinn turned to a clean page of the red notebook and sketched a little map of the area Stillman had wandered in.

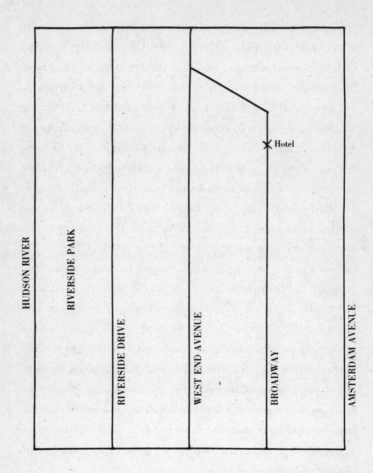

Then, looking carefully through his notes, he began to trace with his pen the movements Stillman had made on a single day—the first day he had kept a full record of the old man's wanderings. The result was as follows:

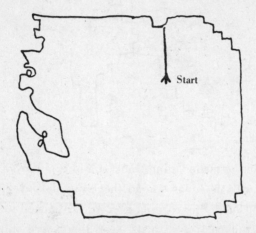

Start

Quinn was struck by the way Stillman had skirted around the edge of the territory, not once venturing into the center. The diagram looked a little like a map of some imaginary state in the Midwest. Except for the eleven blocks up Broadway at the start, and the series of curlicues that represented Stillman's meanderings in Riverside Park, the picture also resembled a rectangle. On the other hand, given the quadrant structure of New York streets, it might also have been a zero or the letter "O."

Quinn went on to the next day and decided to see what would happen. The results were not at all the same.

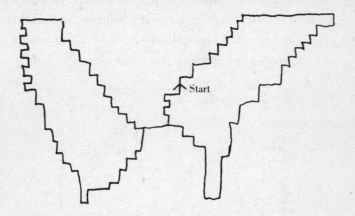

This picture made Quinn think of a bird, a bird of prey perhaps, with its wings spread, hovering aloft in the air. A moment later, this reading seemed far-fetched to him. The bird vanished, and in its stead there were only two abstract shapes, linked by the tiny bridge Stillman had formed by walking west on 83rd Street. Quinn paused for a moment to ponder what he was doing. Was he scribbling nonsense? Was he feeble-mindedly frittering away the evening, or was he trying to find something? Either response, he realized, was unacceptable. If he was simply killing time, why had he chosen such a painstaking way to do it? Was he so muddled that he no longer had the courage to think? On the other hand, if he was not merely diverting himself, what was he actually up to? It seemed to him that he was looking for a sign. He was ransacking the chaos of

Stillman's movements for some glimmer of cogency. This implied only one thing: that he continued to disbelieve the arbitrariness of Stillman's actions. He wanted there to be a sense to them, no matter how obscure. This, in itself, was unacceptable. For it meant that Quinn was allowing himself to deny the facts, and this, as he well knew, was the worst thing a detective could do.

Nevertheless, he decided to go on with it. It was not late, not even eleven o'clock yet, and the truth was that it could do no harm. The results of the third map bore no resemblance to the other two.

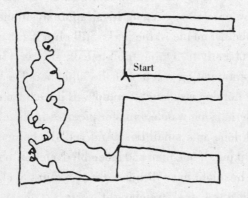

There no longer seemed to be a question about what was happening. If he discounted the squiggles from the park, Quinn felt certain that he was looking at the letter "E." Assuming the first diagram had in fact represented the letter "O," then it seemed legitimate to assume that the bird wings of the second formed the letter "W." Of course, the letters O-W-E spelled a word, but Quinn was not ready to draw any conclusions. He had not begun his inventory until the fifth day of Stillman's travels, and the identities of the first four letters were anyone's guess. He regretted not having started sooner, knowing now that the mystery of those four days was irretrievable. But perhaps he would be able to make up for the past by plunging forward. By coming to the end, perhaps he could intuit the beginning.

The next day's diagram seemed to yield a shape that resembled the letter "R." As with the others, it was complicated by numerous irregularities, approximations, and ornate embellishments in the park. Still clinging to a semblance of objectivity, Quinn tried to look at it as if he had not been anticipating a letter of the alphabet. He had to admit that nothing was sure: it could well have been meaningless. Perhaps he was looking for pictures in the clouds, as he had done as a small boy. And yet, the coincidence was too striking. If one map had resembled a letter, perhaps even two, he might have dismissed it as a quirk of chance. But four in a row was stretching it too far.

The next day gave him a lopsided "O," a doughnut crushed on one side with three or four jagged lines sticking out the other. Then came a tidy "F," with the customary rococo swirls to the side. After that there was a "B" that looked like two boxes haphazardly placed on top of one another, with packing excelsior brimming over the edges. Next there was a tottering "A" that somewhat resembled a ladder, with graded steps on each side. And finally there was a second "B": precariously tilted on a perverse single point, like an upside-down pyramid.

Quinn then copied out the letters in order: OWEROF-BAB. After fiddling with them for a quarter of an hour, switching them around, pulling them apart, rearranging the sequence, he returned to the original order and wrote them out in the following manner: OWER OF BAB. The solution seemed so grotesque that his nerve almost failed him. Making all due allowances for the fact that he had missed the first four days and that Stillman had not yet finished, the answer seemed inescapable: THE TOWER OF BABEL.

Quinn's thoughts momentarily flew off to the concluding pages of *A. Gordon Pym* and to the discovery of the strange hieroglyphs on the inner wall of the chasm—letters inscribed into the earth itself, as though they were trying to say something that could no longer be understood. But on second thought this did not seem apt. For Stillman had not left his message anywhere. True, he had created the letters by the movement of his steps, but they had not been written down. It was like drawing a picture in the air with your finger. The image vanishes as you are making it. There is no result, no trace to mark what you have done.

And yet, the pictures did exist—not in the streets where

they had been drawn, but in Quinn's red notebook. He wondered if Stillman had sat down each night in his room and plotted his course for the following day or whether he had improvised as he had gone along. It was impossible to know. He also wondered what purpose this writing served in Stillman's mind. Was it merely some sort of note to himself, or was it intended as a message to others? At the very least, Quinn concluded, it meant that Stillman had not forgotten Henry Dark.

Quinn did not want to panic. In an effort to restrain himself, he tried to imagine things in the worst possible light. By seeing the worst, perhaps it would not be as bad as he thought. He broke it down as follows. First: Stillman was indeed plotting something against Peter. Response: that had been the premise in any case. Second: Stillman had known he would be followed, had known his movements would be recorded, had known his message would be deciphered. Response: that did not change the essential fact—that Peter had to be protected. Third: Stillman was far more dangerous than previously imagined. Response: that did not mean he could get away with it.

This helped somewhat. But the letters continued to horrify Quinn. The whole thing was so oblique, so fiendish in its circumlocutions, that he did not want to accept it. Then doubts came, as if on command, filling his head with mocking, sing-song voices. He had imagined the whole thing. The letters were not letters at all. He had seen them only because he had wanted to see them. And even if the diagrams did form letters, it was only a fluke. Stillman had nothing to do with it. It was all an accident, a hoax he had perpetrated on himself.

He decided to go to bed, slept fitfully, woke up, wrote in the red notebook for half an hour, went back to bed. His last thought before he went to sleep was that he probably had two more days, since Stillman had not yet completed his message. The last two letters remained—the "E" and the "L." Quinn's mind dispersed. He arrived in a neverland of fragments, a place of wordless things and thingless words. Then, struggling through his torpor one last time, he told himself that El was the ancient Hebrew for God.

In his dream, which he later forgot, he found himself in the town dump of his childhood, sifting through a mountain of rubbish.

9

THE first meeting with Stillman took place in Riverside Park. It was mid-afternoon, a Saturday of bicycles, dog-walkers, and children. Stillman was sitting alone on a bench, staring out at nothing in particular, the little red notebook on his lap. There was light everywhere, an immense light that seemed to radiate outward from each thing the eye caught hold of, and overhead, in the branches of the trees, a breeze continued to blow, shaking the leaves with a passionate hissing, a rising and falling that breathed on as steadily as surf.

Quinn had planned his moves carefully. Pretending not to notice Stillman, he sat down on the bench beside him, folded his arms across his chest, and stared out in the same direction as the old man. Neither of them spoke. By his later calculations, Quinn estimated that this went on for fifteen or twenty minutes. Then, without warning, he turned his head toward the old man and looked at him point–blank, stubbornly fixing his eyes on the wrinkled profile. Quinn concentrated all his strength in his eyes, as if they could begin to burn a hole in Stillman's skull. This stare went on for five minutes.

At last Stillman turned to him. In a surprisingly gentle tenor voice he said, "I'm sorry, but it won't be possible for me to talk to you."

"I haven't said anything," said Quinn.

"That's true," said Stillman. "But you must understand that I'm not in the habit of talking to strangers."

"I repeat," said Quinn, "that I haven't said anything."

"Yes, I heard you the first time. But aren't you interested in knowing why?"

"I'm afraid not."

"Well put. I can see you're a man of sense."

Quinn shrugged, refusing to respond. His whole being now exuded indifference.

Stillman smiled brightly at this, leaned toward Quinn, and said in a conspiratorial voice, "I think we're going to get along."

"That remains to be seen," said Quinn after a long pause.

Stillman laughed—a brief, booming "haw"—and then continued. "It's not that I dislike strangers per se. It's just that I prefer not to speak to anyone who does not introduce himself. In order to begin, I must have a name."

"But once a man gives you his name, he's no longer a stranger."

"Exactly. That's why I never talk to strangers."

Quinn had been prepared for this and knew how to answer. He was not going to let himself be caught. Since he was technically Paul Auster, that was the name he had to protect. Anything else, even the truth, would be an invention, a mask to hide behind and keep him safe.

"In that case," he said, "I'm happy to oblige you. My name is Quinn."

"Ah," said Stillman reflectively, nodding his head. "Quinn."

"Yes, Quinn. Q-U-I-N-N."

"I see. Yes, yes, I see. Quinn. Hmmm. Yes. Very interesting. Quinn. A most resonant word. Rhymes with twin, does it not?"

"That's right. Twin."

"And sin, too, if I'm not mistaken."

"You're not."

"And also in——one n——or inn——two. Isn't that so?"

"Exactly."

"Hmmm. Very interesting. I see many possibilities for this word, this Quinn, this . . . quintessence . . . of quidity. Quick, for example. And quill. And quack. And quirk. Hmmm. Rhymes with grin. Not to speak of kin. Hmmm. Very interesting. And win. And fin. And din. And gin. And pin. And tin. And bin. Hmmm. Even rhymes with djinn. Hmmm. And if you say it right, with been. Hmmm. Yes, very interesting. I like your name enormously, Mr. Quinn. It flies off in so many little directions at once."

"Yes, I've often noticed that myself."

"Most people don't pay attention to such things. They think of words as stones, as great unmovable objects with no life, as monads that never change."

"Stones can change. They can be worn away by wind or water. They can erode. They can be crushed. You can turn them into shards, or gravel, or dust."

"Exactly. I could tell you were a man of sense right away, Mr. Quinn. If you only knew how many people have misunderstood me. My work has suffered because of it. Suffered terribly."

"Your work?"

"Yes, my work. My projects, my investigations, my experiments."

"Ah."

"Yes. But in spite of all the setbacks, I have never really been daunted. At present, for example, I am engaged in one of the most important things I have ever done. If all goes well, I believe I will hold the key to a series of major discoveries."

"The key?"

"Yes, the key. A thing that opens locked doors."

"Ah."

"Of course, for the time being I'm merely collecting data, gathering evidence so to speak. Then I will have to coordinate my findings. It's highly demanding work. You wouldn't believe how hard—especially for a man of my age."

"I can imagine."

"That's right. There's so much to do, and so little time to do it. Every morning I get up at dawn. I have to be outside in all kinds of weather, constantly on the move, forever on my feet, going from one place to the next. It wears me out, you can be sure of that."

"But it's worth it."

"Anything for the truth. No sacrifice is too great."

"Indeed."

"You see, no one has understood what I have understood. I'm the first. I'm the only one. It puts a great burden of responsibility on me."

"The world on your shoulders."

"Yes, so to speak. The world, or what is left of it."

"I hadn't realized it was as bad as that."

"It's that bad. Maybe even worse."

"Ah."

"You see, the world is in fragments, sir. And it's my job to put it back together again."

"You've taken on quite a bit."

"I realize that. But I'm merely looking for the principle. That's well within the scope of one man. If I can lay the foundation, other hands can do the work of restoration itself. The important thing is the premise, the theoretical first step. Unfortunately, there is no one else who can do this."

"Have you made much progress?"

"Enormous strides. In fact, I feel now that I'm on the verge of a significant breakthrough."

"I'm reassured to hear it."

"It's a comforting thought, yes. And it's all because of my cleverness, the dazzling clarity of my mind."

"I don't doubt it."

"You see, I've understood the need to limit myself. To work within a terrain small enough to make all results conclusive."

"The premise of the premise, so to speak."

"That's it, exactly. The principle of the principle, the method of operation. You see, the world is in fragments, sir. Not only have we lost our sense of purpose, we have lost the language whereby we can speak of it. These are no doubt spiritual matters, but they have their analogue in the material world. My brilliant stroke has been to confine myself to physical things, to the immediate and tangible. My motives are lofty, but my work now takes place in the realm of the everyday. That's why I'm so often misunderstood. But no matter. I've learned to shrug these things off.

"An admirable response."

"The only response. The only one worthy of a man of my stature. You see, I am in the process of inventing a new language. With work such as that to do, I can't be bothered by the stupidity of others. In any case, it's all part of the disease I'm trying to cure."

"A new language?"

"Yes. A language that will at last say what we have to say. For our words no longer correspond to the world. When things were whole, we felt confident that our words could express them. But little by little these things have broken apart, shattered, collapsed into chaos. And yet our words have remained the same. They have not adapted themselves to the new reality. Hence, every time we try to speak of what we see, we speak falsely, distorting the very thing we are trying to represent. It's made a mess of everything. But words, as you yourself understand, are capable of change. The problem is how to demonstrate this. That is why I now work with the simplest means possible— so simple that even a child can grasp what I am saying. Consider a word that refers to a thing—'umbrella,' for example. When I say the word 'umbrella,' you see the object in your mind. You see a kind of stick, with collapsible metal spokes on top that form an armature for a waterproof material which, when opened, will protect you from the rain. This last detail is important. Not only is an umbrella a thing, it is a thing that performs a function— in other words, expresses the will of man. When you stop to think of it, every object is similar to the umbrella, in that it serves a function. A pencil is for writing, a shoe is for wearing, a car is for driving. Now, my question is this. What happens when a thing no longer performs its function? Is it still the thing, or has it become something else? When you rip the cloth off the umbrella, is the umbrella still an umbrella? You open the spokes, put them over your head, walk out into the rain, and you get drenched. Is it possible to go on calling this object an umbrella? In general, people do. At the very limit, they will say the umbrella is broken. To me this is a serious error, the source of all our troubles. Because it can no longer perform its function, the umbrella has ceased to be an umbrella. It might resemble an umbrella, it might once have been an umbrella, but now it has changed into something else. The word, however, has remained the same. Therefore, it can no longer express the thing. It is imprecise; it is false; it hides the thing it is supposed to reveal. And if we cannot even name a common, everyday object that we hold in our hands, how can we expect to speak of the things that truly concern us? Unless we can begin to embody the notion of change in the words we use, we will continue to be lost."

"And your work?"

"My work is very simple. I have come to New York because it is the most forlorn of places, the most abject. The brokenness is everywhere, the disarray is universal. You have only to open your eyes to see it. The broken people, the broken things, the broken thoughts. The whole city is a junk heap. It suits my purpose admirably. I find the streets an endless source of material, an inexhaustible storehouse of shattered things. Each day I go out with my bag and collect objects that seem worthy of investigation. My samples now number in the hundreds—from the chipped to the smashed, from the dented to the squashed, from the pulverized to the putrid."

"What do you do with these things?"

"I give them names."

"Names?"

"I invent new words that will correspond to the things."

"Ah. Now I see. But how do you decide? How do you know if you've found the right word?"

"I never make a mistake. It's a function of my genius."

"Could you give me an example?"

"Of one of my words?"

"Yes."

"I'm sorry, but that won't be possible. It's my secret, you understand. Once I've published my book, you and the rest of the world will know. But for now I have to keep it to myself."

"Classified information."

"That's right. Top secret."

"I'm sorry."

"You shouldn't be too disappointed. It won't be long now before I've put my findings in order. Then great things will begin to happen. It will be the most important event in the history of mankind."

●

The second meeting took place a little past nine o'clock the following morning. It was Sunday, and Stillman had emerged from the hotel an hour later than usual. He walked the two blocks to his customary breakfast place, the May-flower Cafe, and sat down in a corner booth at the back. Quinn, growing bolder now, followed the old man into the restaurant and sat down in the same booth, directly opposite him. For a minute or two Stillman seemed not to notice his presence. Then, looking up from his menu, he studied Quinn's face in an abstract sort of way. He apparently did not recognize him from the day before.

"Do I know you?" he asked.

"I don't think so," said Quinn. "My name is Henry Dark."

"Ah," Stillman nodded. "A man who begins with the essential. I like that."

"I'm not one to beat around the bush," said Quinn.

"The bush? What bush might that be?"

"The burning bush, of course."

"Ah, yes. The burning bush. Of course." Stillman looked at Quinn's face—a little more carefully now, but also with what seemed to be a certain confusion. "I'm sorry," he went on, "but I don't remember your name. I recall that you gave it to me not long ago, but now it seems to be gone."

"Henry Dark," said Quinn.

"So it is. Yes, now it comes back to me. Henry Dark."
Stillman paused for a long moment and then shook his
head. "Unfortunately, that's not possible, sir."

"Why not?"

"Because there is no Henry Dark."

"Well, perhaps I'm another Henry Dark. As opposed to
the one who doesn't exist."

"Hmmm. Yes, I see your point. It is true that two people
sometimes have the same name. It's quite possible that
your name is Henry Dark. But you're not *the* Henry Dark."

"Is he a friend of yours?"

Stillman laughed, as if at a good joke. "Not exactly,"
he said. "You see, there never was any such person as
Henry Dark. I made him up. He's an invention."

"No," said Quinn, with feigned disbelief.

"Yes. He's a character in a book I once wrote. A fig-
ment."

"I find that hard to accept."

"So did everyone else. I fooled them all."

"Amazing. Why in the world did you do it?"

"I needed him, you see. I had certain ideas at the time
that were too dangerous and controversial. So I pretended
they had come from someone else. It was a way of protecting myself."

"How did you decide on the name Henry Dark?"

"It's a good name, don't you think? I like it very much.

Full of mystery, and at the same time quite proper. It suited my purpose well. And besides, it had a secret meaning."

"The allusion to darkness?"

"No, no. Nothing so obvious. It was the initials, H.D. That was very important."

"How so?"

"Don't you want to guess?"

"I don't think so."

"Oh, do try. Make three guesses. If you don't get it, then I'll tell you."

Quinn paused for a moment, trying to give it his best effort. "H.D.," he said. "For Henry David? As in Henry David Thoreau."

"Not even close."

"How about H.D. pure and simple? For the poet Hilda Doolittle."

"Worse than the first one."

"All right, one more guess. H.D.H. . . . and D. . . . Just a moment. . . . How about. . . . Just a moment. . . . Ah. . . . Yes, here we are. H for the weeping philosopher, Heraclitus . . . and D for the laughing philosopher, Democritus. Heraclitus and Democritus . . . the two poles of the dialectic."

"A very clever answer."

"Am I right?"

"No, of course not. But a clever answer just the same."

"You can't say I didn't try."

"No, I can't. That's why I'm going to reward you with the correct answer. Because you tried. Are you ready?"

"Ready."

"The initials H. D. in the name Henry Dark refer to Humpty Dumpty."

"Who?"

"Humpty Dumpty. You know who I mean. The egg."

"As in 'Humpty Dumpty sat on a wall'?"

"Exactly."

"I don't understand."

"Humpty Dumpty: the purest embodiment of the human condition. Listen carefully, sir. What is an egg? It is that which has not yet been born. A paradox, is it not? For how can Humpty Dumpty be alive if he has not been born? And yet, he is alive—make no mistake. We know that because he can speak. More than that, he is a philosopher of language. 'When *I* use a word, Humpty Dumpty said, in rather a scornful tone, it means just what I choose it to mean—neither more nor less. The question is, said Alice, whether you *can* make words mean so many different things. The question is, said Humpty Dumpty, which is to be master—that's all.' "

"Lewis Carroll."

"*Through the Looking Glass*, chapter six."

"Interesting."

"It's more than interesting, sir. It's crucial. Listen carefully, and perhaps you will learn something. In his little speech to Alice, Humpty Dumpty sketches the future of human hopes and gives the clue to our salvation: to become masters of the words we speak, to make language answer our needs, Humpty Dumpty was a prophet, a man who spoke truths the world was not ready for."

"A man?"

"Excuse me. A slip of the tongue. I mean an egg. But the slip is instructive and helps to prove my point. For all men are eggs, in a manner of speaking. We exist, but we have not yet achieved the form that is our destiny. We are pure potential, an example of the not-yet-arrived. For man is a fallen creature—we know that from Genesis. Humpty Dumpty is also a fallen creature. He falls from his wall, and no one can put him back together again—neither the king, nor his horses, nor his men. But that is what we must all now strive to do. It is our duty as human beings: to put the egg back together again. For each of us, sir, is Humpty Dumpty. And to help him is to help ourselves."

"A convincing argument."

"It's impossible to find a flaw in it."

"No cracks in the egg."

"Exactly."

"And, at the same time, the origin of Henry Dark."

"Yes. But there is more to it than that. Another egg, in fact."

"There's more than one?"

"Good heavens, yes. There are millions of them. But the one I have in mind is particularly famous. It's probably the most celebrated egg of all."

"You're beginning to lose me."

"I'm speaking of Columbus's egg."

"Ah, yes. Of course."

"You know the story?"

"Everyone does."

"It's charming, is it not? When faced with the problem of how to stand an egg on its end, he merely tapped slightly on the bottom, cracking the shell just enough to create a certain flatness that would support the egg when he removed his hand."

"It worked."

"Of course it worked. Columbus was a genius. He sought paradise and discovered the New World. It is still not too late for it to become paradise."

"Indeed."

"I admit that things have not worked out too well yet. But there is still hope. Americans have never lost their desire to discover new worlds. Do you remember what happened in 1969?"

"I remember many things. What do you have in mind?"

"Men walked on the moon. Think of that, dear sir. Men walked on the moon!"

"Yes, I remember. According to the President, it was the greatest event since creation."

"He was right. The only intelligent thing that man ever said. And what do you suppose the moon looks like?"

"I have no idea."

"Come, come, think again."

"Oh yes. Now I see what you mean."

"Granted, the resemblance is not perfect. But it is true that in certain phases, especially on a clear night, the moon does look very much like an egg."

"Yes. Very much like."

At that moment, a waitress appeared with Stillman's breakfast and set it on the table before him. The old man eyed the food with relish. Decorously lifting a knife with his right hand, he cracked the shell of his soft-boiled egg and said, "As you can see, sir, I leave no stone unturned."

The third meeting took place later that same day. The afternoon was well advanced: the light like gauze on the bricks and leaves, the shadows lengthening. Once again, Stillman retreated to Riverside Park, this time to the edge of it, coming to rest on a knobby outcrop at 84th Street known as Mount Tom. On this same spot, in the summers of 1843 and 1844, Edgar Allan Poe had spent many long hours gazing out at the Hudson. Quinn knew this because he had made it his business to know such things. As it turned out, he had often sat there himself.

He felt little fear now about doing what he had to do. He circled the rock two or three times, but failed to get

Stillman's attention. Then he sat down next to the old man and said hello. Incredibly, Stillman did not recognize him. This was the third time Quinn had presented himself, and each time it was as though Quinn had been someone else. He could not decide whether this was a good sign or bad. If Stillman was pretending, he was an actor like no other in the world. For each time Quinn had appeared, he had done it by surprise. And yet Stillman had not even blinked. On the other hand, if Stillman really did not recognize him, what did this mean? Was it possible for anyone to be so impervious to the things he saw?

The old man asked him who he was.

"My name is Peter Stillman," said Quinn.

"That's my name," answered Stillman. "I'm Peter Stillman."

"I'm the other Peter Stillman," said Quinn.

"Oh. You mean my son. Yes, that's possible. You look just like him. Of course, Peter is blond and you are dark. Not Henry Dark, but dark of hair. But people change, don't they? One minute we're one thing, and then another another."

"Exactly."

"I've often wondered about you, Peter. Many times I've thought to myself, 'I wonder how Peter is getting along.' "

"I'm much better now, thank you."

"I'm glad to hear it. Someone once told me you had died. It made me very sad."

"No, I've made a complete recovery."

"I can see that. Fit as a fiddle. And you speak so well, too."

"All words are available to me now. Even the ones most people have trouble with. I can say them all."

"I'm proud of you, Peter."

"I owe it all to you."

"Children are a great blessing. I've always said that. An incomparable blessing."

"I'm sure of it."

"As for me, I have my good days and my bad days. When the bad days come, I think of the ones that were good. Memory is a great blessing, Peter. The next best thing to death."

"Without a doubt."

"Of course, we must live in the present, too. For example, I am currently in New York. Tomorrow, I could be somewhere else. I travel a great deal, you see. Here today, gone tomorrow. It's part of my work."

"It must be stimulating."

"Yes, I'm very stimulated. My mind never stops."

"That's good to hear."

"The years weigh heavily, it's true. But we have so much to be thankful for. Time makes us grow old, but it also gives us the day and the night. And when we die, there is always someone to take our place."

"We all grow old."

"When you're old, perhaps you'll have a son to comfort you."

"I would like that."

"Then you would be as fortunate as I have been. Remember, Peter, children are a great blessing."

"I won't forget."

"And remember, too, that you shouldn't put all your eggs in one basket. Conversely, don't count your chickens before they hatch."

"No. I try to take things as they come."

"Last of all, never say a thing you know in your heart is not true."

"I won't."

"Lying is a bad thing. It makes you sorry you were ever born. And not to have been born is a curse. You are condemned to live outside time. And when you live outside time, there is no day and night. You don't even get a chance to die."

"I understand."

"A lie can never be undone. Even the truth is not enough. I am a father, and I know about these things. Remember what happened to the father of our country. He chopped down the cherry tree, and then he said to his father, 'I cannot tell a lie.' Soon thereafter, he threw the coin across the river. These two stories are crucial events in American history. George Washington chopped down the tree, and then he threw away the money. Do you understand? He was telling us an essential truth. Namely, that money doesn't grow on trees. This is what made our country great, Peter. Now George Washington's picture is on every dollar bill. There is an important lesson to be learned from all this."

"I agree with you."

"Of course, it's unfortunate that the tree was cut down. That tree was the Tree of Life, and it would have made us immune to death. Now we welcome death with open arms, especially when we are old. But the father of our country knew his duty. He could not do otherwise. That is the meaning of the phrase 'Life is a bowl of cherries.' If the tree had remained standing, we would have had eternal life."

"Yes, I see what you mean."

"I have many such ideas in my head. My mind never stops. You were always a clever boy, Peter, and I'm glad you understand."

"I can follow you perfectly."

"A father must always teach his son the lessons he has learned. In that way knowledge is passed down from generation to generation, and we grow wise."

"I won't forget what you've told me."

"I'll be able to die happily now, Peter."

"I'm glad."

"But you musn't forget anything."

"I won't, father. I promise."

●

The next morning, Quinn was in front of the hotel at his usual time. The weather had finally changed. After two weeks of resplendent skies, a drizzle now fell on New York, and the streets were filled with the sound of wet, moving tires. For an hour Quinn sat on the bench, protecting himself with a black umbrella, thinking Stillman would appear at any moment. He worked his way through his roll and coffee, read the account of the Mets' Sunday loss, and still there was no sign of the old man. Patience, he said to himself, and began to tackle the rest of the paper. Forty minutes passed. He reached the financial section and was about to read an analysis of a corporate merger when the rain suddenly intensified. Reluctantly, he got up from his bench and removed himself to a doorway across the street from the hotel. He stood there in his clammy shoes for an hour and a half. Was Stillman sick? he wondered. Quinn tried to imagine him lying in his bed, sweating out a fever. Perhaps the old man had died during the night and his body had not yet been discovered. Such things happened, he told himself.

Today was to have been the crucial day, and Quinn had made elaborate and meticulous plans for it. Now his calculations were for naught. It disturbed him that he had not taken this contingency into account.

Still, he hesitated. He stood there under his umbrella, watching the rain slide off it in small, fine drops. By eleven o'clock he had begun to formulate a decision. Half an hour later he crossed the street, walked forty paces down the block, and entered Stillman's hotel. The place stank of cockroach repellant and dead cigarettes. A few of the tenants, with nowhere to go in the rain, were sitting in the lobby, sprawled out on orange plastic chairs. The place seemed blank, a hell of stale thoughts.

A large black man sat behind the front desk with his sleeves rolled up. One elbow was on the counter, and his head was propped in his open hand. With his other hand he turned the pages of a tabloid newspaper, barely pausing to read the words. He looked bored enough to have been there all his life.

"I'd like to leave a message for one of your guests," Quinn said.

The man looked up at him slowly, as if wishing him to disappear.

"I'd like to leave a message for one of your guests," Quinn said again.

"No guests here," said the man. "We call them residents."

"For one of your residents, then. I'd like to leave a message."

"And just who might that be, bub?"

"Stillman. Peter Stillman."

The man pretended to think for a moment, then shook his head. "Nope. Can't recall anyone by that name."

"Don't you have a register?"

"Yeah, we've got a book. But it's in the safe."

"The safe? What are you talking about?"

"I'm talking about the book, bub. The boss likes to keep it locked up in the safe."

"I don't suppose you know the combination?"

"Sorry. The boss is the only one."

Quinn sighed, reached into his pocket, and pulled out a five-dollar bill. He slapped it on the counter and kept his hand on top of it.

"I don't suppose you happen to have a copy of the book, do you?" he asked.

"Maybe," said the man. "I'll have to look in my office."

The man lifted up the newspaper, which was lying open on the counter. Under it was the register.

"A lucky break," said Quinn, releasing his hand from the money.

"Yeah, I guess today's my day," answered the man, sliding the bill along the surface of the counter, whisking it over the edge, and putting it in his pocket. "What did you say your friend's name was again?"

"Stillman. An old man with white hair."

"The gent in the overcoat?"

"That's right."

"We call him the Professor."

"That's the man. Do you have a room number? He checked in about two weeks ago."

The clerk opened the register, turned the pages, and ran his finger down the column of names and numbers. "Stillman," he said. "Room 303. He's not here anymore."

"What?"

"He checked out."

"What are you talking about?"

"Listen, bub, I'm only telling you what it says here. Stillman checked out last night. He's gone."

"That's the craziest thing I ever heard."

"I don't care what it is. It's all down here in black and white."

"Did he give a forwarding address?"

"Are you kidding?"

"What time did he leave?"

"Have to ask Louie, the night man. He comes on at eight."

"Can I see the room?"

"Sorry. I rented it myself this morning. The guy's up there asleep."

"What did he look like?"

"For five bucks you've got a lot of questions."

"Forget it," said Quinn, waving his hand desperately. "It doesn't matter."

He walked back to his apartment in a downpour, getting drenched in spite of his umbrella. So much for functions, he said to himself. So much for the meaning of words. He threw the umbrella onto the floor of his living room in disgust. Then he took off his jacket and flung it against the wall. Water splattered everywhere.

He called Virginia Stillman, too embarrassed to think of doing anything else. At the moment she answered, he nearly hung up the phone.

"I lost him," he said.

"Are you sure?"

"He checked out of his room last night. I don't know where he is."

"I'm scared, Paul."

"Have you heard from him?"

"I don't know. I think so, but I'm not sure."

"What does that mean?"

"Peter answered the phone this morning while I was taking my bath. He won't tell me who it was. He went into his room, closed the shades, and refuses to speak."

"But he's done that before."

"Yes. That's why I'm not sure. But it hasn't happened in a long time."

"It sounds bad."

"That's what I'm afraid of."

"Don't worry. I have a few ideas. I'll get to work on them right away."

"How will I reach you?"

"I'll call you every two hours, no matter where I am."

"Do you promise?"

"Yes, I promise."

"I'm so scared, I can't stand it."

"It's all my fault. I made a stupid mistake, and I'm sorry."

"No, I don't blame you. No one can watch a person twenty-four hours a day. It's impossible. You'd have to be inside his skin."

"That's just the trouble. I thought I was."

"It's not too late now, is it?"

"No. There's still plenty of time. I don't want you to worry."

"I'll try not to."

"Good. I'll be in touch."

"Every two hours?"

"Every two hours."

He had finessed the conversation rather nicely. In spite of everything, he had managed to keep Virginia Stillman calm. He found it hard to believe, but she still seemed to trust him. Not that it would be of any help. For the fact was, he had lied to her. He did not have several ideas. He did not have even one.

10

STILLMAN was gone now. The old man had become part of the city. He was a speck, a punctuation mark, a brick in an endless wall of bricks. Quinn could walk through the streets every day for the rest of his life, and still he would not find him. Everything had been reduced to chance, a nightmare of numbers and probabilities. There were no clues, no leads, no moves to be made.

Quinn backtracked in his mind to the beginning of the case. His job had been to protect Peter, not to follow Stillman. That had simply been a method, a way of trying to predict what would happen. By watching Stillman, the theory was that he would learn what his intentions were toward Peter. He had followed the old man for two weeks. What, then, could he conclude? Not much. Stillman's behavior had been too obscure to give any hints.

There were, of course, certain extreme measures that they could take. He could suggest to Virginia Stillman that she get an unlisted telephone number. That would eliminate the disturbing calls, at least temporarily. If that failed, she and Peter could move. They could leave the neighborhood, perhaps leave the city altogether. At the very worst, they could take on new identities, live under different names.

This last thought reminded him of something important. Until now, he realized, he had never seriously questioned the circumstances of his hiring. Things had happened too quickly, and he had taken it for granted that he could fill in for Paul Auster. Once he had taken the leap into that name, he had stopped thinking about Auster himself. If this man was as good a detective as the Stillmans thought he was, perhaps he would be able to help with the case. Quinn would make a clean breast of it, Auster would forgive him, and together they would work to save Peter Stillman.

He looked through the yellow pages for the Auster Detective Agency. There was no listing. In the white pages, however, he found the name. There was one Paul Auster in Manhattan, living on Riverside Drive—not far from Quinn's own house. There was no mention of a detective agency, but that did not necessarily mean anything. It could be that Auster had so much work he didn't need to advertise. Quinn picked up the phone and was about to dial when he thought better of it. This was too important a conversation to leave to the phone. He did not want to run the risk of being brushed off. Since Auster did not have an office, that meant he worked at home. Quinn would go there and talk to him face to face.

The rain had stopped now, and although the sky was

still gray, far to the west Quinn could see a tiny shaft of light seeping through the clouds. As he walked up Riverside Drive, he became aware of the fact that he was no longer following Stillman. It felt as though he had lost half of himself. For two weeks he had been tied by an invisible thread to the old man. Whatever Stillman had done, he had done; wherever Stillman had gone, he had gone. His body was not accustomed to this new freedom, and for the first few blocks he walked at the old shuffling pace. The spell was over, and yet his body did not know it.

Auster's building was in the middle of the long block that ran between 116th and 119th Streets, just south of Riverside Church and Grant's Tomb. It was a well-kept place, with polished doorknobs and clean glass, and it had an air of bourgeois sobriety that appealed to Quinn at that moment. Auster's apartment was on the eleventh floor, and Quinn rang the buzzer, expecting to hear a voice speak to him through the intercom. But the door buzzer answered him without any conversation. Quinn pushed the door open, walked through the lobby, and rode the elevator to the eleventh floor.

It was a man who opened the apartment door. He was a tall dark fellow in his mid-thirties, with rumpled clothes and a two-day beard. In this right hand, fixed between his thumb and first two fingers, he held an uncapped fountain pen, still poised in a writing position. The man seemed surprised to find a stranger standing before him.

"Yes?" he asked tentatively.

Quinn spoke in the politest tone he could muster. "Were you expecting someone else?"

"My wife, as a matter of fact. That's why I rang the buzzer without asking who it was."

"I'm sorry to disturb you," Quinn apologized. "But I'm looking for Paul Auster."

"I'm Paul Auster," said the man.

"I wonder if I could talk to you. It's quite important."

"You'll have to tell me what it's about first."

"I hardly know myself." Quinn gave Auster an earnest look. "It's complicated, I'm afraid. Very complicated."

"Do you have a name?"

"I'm sorry. Of course I do. Quinn."

"Quinn what?"

"Daniel Quinn."

The name seemed to suggest something to Auster, and he paused for a moment abstractedly, as if searching through his memory. "Quinn," he muttered to himself. "I know that name from somewhere." He went silent again, straining harder to dredge up the answer. "You aren't a poet, are you?"

"I used to be," said Quinn. "But I haven't written poems for a long time now."

"You did a book several years ago, didn't you? I think the title was *Unfinished Business*. A little book with a blue cover."

"Yes. That was me."

"I liked it very much. I kept hoping to see more of your work. In fact, I even wondered what had happened to you."

"I'm still here. Sort of."

Auster opened the door wider and gestured for Quinn to enter the apartment. It was a pleasant enough place inside: oddly shaped, with several long corridors, books cluttered everywhere, pictures on the walls by artists Quinn did not know, and a few children's toys scattered on the floor—a red truck, a brown bear, a green space monster. Auster led him to the living room, gave him a frayed upholstered chair to sit in, and then went off to the kitchen to fetch some beer. He returned with two bottles, placed them on a wooden crate that served as the coffee table, and sat down on the sofa across from Quinn.

"Was it some kind of literary thing you wanted to talk about?" Auster began.

"No," said Quinn. "I wish it was. But this has nothing to do with literature."

"With what, then?"

Quinn paused, looked around the room without seeing anything, and tried to start. "I have a feeling there's been a terrible mistake. I came here looking for Paul Auster, the private detective."

"The what?" Auster laughed, and in that laugh everything was suddenly blown to bits. Quinn realized that he was talking nonsense. He might just as well have asked for Chief Sitting Bull—the effect would have been no different.

"The private detective," he repeated softly.

"I'm afraid you've got the wrong Paul Auster."

"You're the only one in the book."

"That might be," said Auster. "But I'm not a detective."

"Who are you then? What do you do?"

"I'm a writer."

"A writer?" Quinn spoke the word as though it were a lament.

"I'm sorry," Auster said. "But that's what I happen to be."

"If that's true, then there's no hope. The whole thing is a bad dream."

"I have no idea what you're talking about."

Quinn told him. He began at the beginning and went through the entire story, step by step. The pressure had been building up in him since Stillman's disappearance that morning, and it came out of him now as a torrent of words. He told of the phone calls for Paul Auster, of his inexplicable acceptance of the case, of his meeting with Peter Stillman, of his conversation with Virginia Stillman, of his reading Stillman's book, of his following Stillman from Grand Central Station, of Stillman's daily wanderings, of the carpet bag and the broken objects, of the disquieting maps that formed letters of the alphabet, of his talks with Stillman, of Stillman's disappearance from the hotel. When he had come to the end, he said, "Do you think I'm crazy?"

"No," said Auster, who had listened attentively to Quinn's monologue. "If I had been in your place, I probably would have done the same thing."

These words came as a great relief to Quinn, as if, at long last, the burden was no longer his alone. He felt like taking Auster in his arms and declaring his friendship for life.

"You see," said Quinn, "I'm not making it up. I even have proof." He took out his wallet and removed the five-hundred-dollar check that Virginia Stillman had written two weeks earlier. He handed it to Auster. "You see," he said. "It's even made out to you."

Auster looked the check over carefully and nodded. "It's seems to be a perfectly normal check."

"Well, it's yours," said Quinn. "I want you to have it."

"I couldn't possibly accept it."

"It's of no use to me." Quinn looked around the apartment and gestured vaguely. "Buy yourself some more books. Or a few toys for your kid."

"This is money you've earned. You deserve to have it yourself." Auster paused for a moment. "There's one thing I'll do for you, though. Since the check is in my name, I'll cash it for you. I'll take it to my bank tomorrow morning, deposit it in my account, and give you the money when it clears."

Quinn did not say anything.

"All right?" Auster asked. "Is it agreed?"

"All right," said Quinn at last. "We'll see what happens."

Auster put the check on the coffee table, as if to say the matter had been settled. Then he leaned back on the sofa and looked Quinn in the eyes. "There's a much more important question than the check," he said. "The fact that my name has been mixed up in this. I don't understand it at all."

"I wonder if you've had any trouble with your phone lately. Wires sometimes get crossed. A person tries to call a number, and even though he dials correctly, he gets someone else."

"Yes, that's happened to me before. But even if my phone was broken, that doesn't explain the real problem. It would tell us why the call went to you, but not why they wanted to speak to me in the first place."

"Is it possible that you know the people involved?"

"I've never heard of the Stillmans."

"Maybe someone wanted to play a practical joke on you."

"I don't hang around with people like that."

"You never know."

"But the fact is, it's not a joke. It's a real case with real people."

"Yes," said Quinn after a long silence. "I'm aware of that."

They had come to the end of what they could talk about. Beyond that point there was nothing: the random thoughts of men who knew nothing. Quinn realized that he should be going. He had been there almost an hour, and the time was approaching for his call to Virginia Stillman. Nevertheless, he was reluctant to move. The chair was comfortable, and the beer had gone slightly to his head. This Auster was the first intelligent person he had spoken to in a long time. He had read Quinn's old work, he had admired it, he had been looking forward to more. In spite of everything, it was impossible for Quinn not to feel glad of this.

They sat there for a short time without saying anything. At last, Auster gave a little shrug, which seemed to acknowledge that they had come to an impasse. He stood up and said, "I was about to make some lunch for myself. It's no trouble making it for two."

Quinn hesitated. It was as though Auster had read his thoughts, divining the thing he wanted most—to eat, to have an excuse to stay a while. "I really should be going," he said. "But yes, thank you. A little food can't do any harm."

"How does a ham omelette sound?"

"Sounds good."

Auster retreated to the kitchen to prepare the food.
Quinn would have liked to offer to help, but he could not
budge. His body felt like a stone. For want of any other
idea, he closed his eyes. In the past, it had sometimes
comforted him to make the world disappear. This time,
however, Quinn found nothing interesting inside his head.
It seemed as though things had ground to a halt in there.
Then, from the darkness, he began to hear a voice, a
chanting, idiotic voice that sang the same sentence over
and over again: "You can't make an omelette without breaking
eggs." He opened his eyes to make the words stop.

There was bread and butter, more beer, knives and
forks, salt and pepper, napkins, and omelettes, two of
them, oozing on white plates. Quinn ate with crude intensity, polishing off the meal in what seemed a matter of
seconds. After that, he made a great effort to be calm.
Tears lurked mysteriously behind his eyes, and his voice
seemed to tremble as he spoke, but somehow he managed
to hold his own. To prove that he was not a self-obsessed
ingrate, he began to question Auster about his writing.
Auster was somewhat reticent about it, but at last he con-
ceded that he was working on a book of essays. The current
piece was about *Don Quixote*.

"One of my favorite books," said Quinn.

"Yes, mine too. There's nothing like it."

Quinn asked him about the essay.

"I suppose you could call it speculative, since I'm not

really out to prove anything. In fact, it's all done tongue-in-cheek. An imaginative reading, I guess you could say."

"What's the gist?"

"It mostly has to do with the authorship of the book. Who wrote it, and how it was written."

"Is there any question?"

"Of course not. But I mean the book inside the book Cervantes wrote, the one he imagined he was writing."

"Ah."

"It's quite simple. Cervantes, if you remember, goes to great lengths to convince the reader that he is not the author. The book, he says, was written in Arabic by Cid Hamete Benengeli. Cervantes describes how he discovered the manuscript by chance one day in the market at Toledo. He hires someone to translate it for him into Spanish, and thereafter he presents himself as no more than the editor of the translation. In fact, he cannot even vouch for the accuracy of the translation itself."

"And yet he goes on to say," Quinn added, "that Cid Hamete Benengeli's is the only true version of Don Quixote's story. All the other versions are frauds, written by imposters. He makes a great point of insisting that everything in the book really happened in the world."

"Exactly. Because the book after all is an attack on the dangers of the make-believe. He couldn't very well offer a work of the imagination to do that, could he? He had to claim that it was real."

"Still, I've always suspected that Cervantes devoured those old romances. You can't hate something so violently unless a part of you also loves it. In some sense, Don Quixote was just a stand-in for himself."

"I agree with you. What better portrait of a writer than to show a man who has been bewitched by books?"

"Precisely."

"In any case, since the book is supposed to be real, it follows that the story has to be written by an eyewitness to the events that take place in it. But Cid Hamete, the acknowledged author, never makes an appearance. Not once does he claim to be present at what happens. So, my question is this: who is Cid Hamete Benengeli?"

"Yes, I see what you're getting at."

"The theory I present in the essay is that he is actually a combination of four different people. Sancho Panza is of course the witness. There's no other candidate—since he is the only one who accompanies Don Quixote on all his adventures. But Sancho can neither read nor write. Therefore, he cannot be the author. On the other hand, we know that Sancho has a great gift for language. In spite of his inane malapropisms, he can talk circles around everyone else in the book. It seems perfectly possible to me that he dictated the story to someone else—namely, to the barber and the priest, Don Quixote's good friends. They put the story into proper literary form—in Spanish—and then turned the manuscript over to Samson Carrasco, the bachelor from

Salamanca, who proceeded to translate it into Arabic. Cervantes found the translation, had it rendered back into Spanish, and then published the book *The Adventures of Don Quixote*."

"But why would Sancho and the others go to all that trouble?"

"To cure Don Quixote of his madness. They want to save their friend. Remember, in the beginning they burn his books of chivalry, but that has no effect. The Knight of the Sad Countenance does not give up his obsession. Then, at one time or another, they all go out looking for him in various disguises—as a woman in distress, as the Knight of the Mirrors, as the Knight of the White Moon—in order to lure Don Quixote back home. In the end, they are actually successful. The book was just one of their ploys. The idea was to hold a mirror up to Don Quixote's madness, to record each of his absurd and ludicrous delusions, so that when he finally read the book himself, he would see the error of his ways."

"I like that."

"Yes. But there's one last twist. Don Quixote, in my view, was not really mad. He only pretended to be. In fact, he orchestrated the whole thing himself. Remember: throughout the book Don Quixote is preoccupied by the question of posterity. Again and again he wonders how accurately his chronicler will record his adventures. This implies knowledge on his part; he knows beforehand that this chronicler exists. And who else is it but Sancho Panza, the faithful squire whom Don Quixote has chosen for exactly this purpose? In the same way, he chose the three others to play the roles he destined for them. It was Don Quixote who engineered the Benengeli quartet. And not only did he select the authors, it was probably he who translated the Arabic manuscript back into Spanish. We shouldn't put it past him. For a man so skilled in the art of disguise, darkening his skin and donning the clothes of a Moor could not have been very difficult. I like to imagine that scene in the marketplace at Toledo. Cervantes hiring Don Quixote to decipher the story of Don Quixote himself. There's great beauty to it."

"But you still haven't explained why a man like Don Quixote would disrupt his tranquil life to engage in such an elaborate hoax."

"That's the most interesting part of all. In my opinion, Don Quixote was conducting an experiment. He wanted to test the gullibility of his fellow men. Would it be possible, he wondered, to stand up before the world and with the utmost conviction spew out lies and nonsense? To say that windmills were knights, that a barber's basin was a helmet, that puppets were real people? Would it be possible to persuade others to agree with what he said, even though they did not believe him? In other words, to what extent would people tolerate blasphemies if they gave them amusement? The answer is obvious, isn't it? To any extent.

For the proof is that we still read the book. It remains highly amusing to us. And that's finally all anyone wants out of a book—to be amused."

Auster leaned back on the sofa, smiled with a certain ironic pleasure, and lit a cigarette. The man was obviously enjoying himself, but the precise nature of that pleasure eluded Quinn. It seemed to be a kind of soundless laughter, a joke that stopped short of its punchline, a generalized mirth that had no object. Quinn was about to say something in response to Auster's theory, but he was not given the chance. Just as he opened his mouth to speak, he was interrupted by a clattering of keys at the front door, the sound of the door opening and then slamming shut, and a burst of voices. Auster's face perked up at the sound. He rose from his seat, excused himself to Quinn, and walked quickly towards the door.

Quinn heard laughter in the hallway, first from a woman and then from a child—the high and the higher, a staccato of ringing shrapnel—and then the basso rumbling of Auster's guffaw. The child spoke: "Daddy, look what I found!" And then the woman explained that it had been lying on the street, and why not, it seemed perfectly okay. A moment later he heard the child running towards him down the hall. The child shot into the living room, caught sight of Quinn, and stopped dead in his tracks. He was a blond-haired boy of five or six.

"Good afternoon," said Quinn.

The boy, rapidly withdrawing into shyness, managed no more than a faint hello. In his left hand he held a red object that Quinn could not identify. Quinn asked the boy what it was.

"It's a yoyo," he answered, opening his hand to show him. "I found it on the street."

"Does it work?"

The boy gave an exaggerated pantomine shrug. "Dunno. Siri can't do it. And I don't know how."

Quinn asked him if he could try, and the boy walked over and put it in his hand. As he examined the yoyo, he could hear the child breathing beside him, watching his every move. The yoyo was plastic, similar to the ones he had played with years ago, but more elaborate somehow, an artifact of the space age. Quinn fastened the loop at the end of the string around his middle finger, stood up, and gave it a try. The yoyo gave off a fluted, whistling sound as it descended, and sparks shot off inside it. The boy gasped, but then the yoyo stopped, dangling at the end of its line.

"A great philosopher once said," muttered Quinn, "that the way up and the way down are one and the same."

"But you didn't make it go up," said the boy. "It only went down."

"You have to keep trying."

Quinn was rewinding the spool for another attempt when Auster and his wife entered the room. He looked up and saw the woman first. In that one brief moment he knew that he was in trouble. She was a tall, thin blonde, radiantly beautiful, with an energy and happiness that seemed to make everything around her invisible. It was too much for Quinn. He felt as though Auster were taunting him with the things he had lost, and he responded with envy and rage, a lacerating self-pity. Yes, he too would have liked to have this wife and this child, to sit around all day spouting drivel about old books, to be surrounded by yoyos and ham omelettes and fountain pens. He prayed to himself for deliverance.

Auster saw the yoyo in his hand and said, "I see you've already met. Daniel," he said to the boy, "this is Daniel." And then to Quinn, with that same ironic smile, "Daniel, this is Daniel."

The boy burst out laughing and said, "Everybody's Daniel!"

"That's right," said Quinn. "I'm you, and you're me."

"And around and around it goes," shouted the boy, suddenly spreading his arms and spinning around the room like a gyroscope.

"And this," said Auster, turning to the woman, "is my wife, Siri."

The wife smiled her smile, said she was glad to meet Quinn as though she meant it, and then extended her hand to him. He shook it, feeling the uncanny slenderness of her bones, and asked if her name was Norwegian.

"Not many people know that," she said.

"Do you come from Norway?"

"Indirectly," she said. "By way of Northfield, Minnesota." And then she laughed her laugh, and Quinn felt a little more of himself collapse.

"I know this is sort of last minute," Auster said, "but if you have some time to spare, why don't you stay and have dinner with us?"

"Ah," said Quinn, struggling to keep himself in check. "That's very kind. But I really must be going. I'm late as it is."

He made one last effort, smiling at Auster's wife and waving good-bye to the boy. "So long, Daniel," he said, walking towards the door.

The boy looked at him from across the room and laughed again. "Good-bye myself!" he said.

Auster accompanied him to the door. He said, "I'll call you as soon as the check clears. Are you in the book?"

"Yes," said Quinn. "The only one."

"If you need me for anything," said Auster, "just call. I'll be happy to help."

Auster reached out to shake hands with him, and Quinn realized that he was still holding the yoyo. He placed it in Auster's right hand, patted him gently on the shoulder, and left.

11

QUINN was nowhere now. He had nothing, he knew nothing, he knew that he knew nothing. Not only had he been sent back to the beginning, he was now before the beginning, and so far before the beginning that it was worse than any end he could imagine.

His watch read nearly six. Quinn walked home the way he had come, lengthening his strides with each new block. By the time he came to his street, he was running. It's June second, he told himself. Try to remember that. This is New York, and tomorrow will be June third. If all goes well, the following day will be the fourth. But nothing is certain.

The hour had long since passed for his call to Virginia Stillman, and he debated whether to go through with it. Would it be possible to ignore her? Could he abandon everything now, just like that? Yes, he said to himself, it was possible. He could forget about the case, get back to his routine, write another book. He could take a trip if he liked, even leave the country for a while. He could go to

Paris, for example. Yes, that was possible. But anywhere would do, he thought, anywhere at all.

He sat down in his living room and looked at the walls. They had once been white, he remembered, but now they had turned a curious shade of yellow. Perhaps one day they would drift further into dinginess, lapsing into gray, or even brown, like some piece of aging fruit. A white wall becomes a yellow wall becomes a gray wall, he said to himself. The paint becomes exhausted, the city encroaches with its soot, the plaster crumbles within. Changes, then more changes still.

He smoked a cigarette, and then another, and then another. He looked at his hands, saw that they were dirty, and got up to wash them. In the bathroom, with the water running in the sink, he decided to shave as well. He lathered his face, took out a clean blade, and started scraping off his beard. For some reason, he found it unpleasant to look in the mirror and kept trying to avoid himself with his eyes. You're getting old, he said to himself, you're turning into an old fart. Then he went into the kitchen, ate a bowl of cornflakes, and smoked another cigarette.

It was seven o'clock now. Once again, he debated whether to call Virginia Stillman. As he turned the question over in his mind, it occurred to him that he no longer had an opinion. He saw the argument for making the call, and at the same time he saw the argument for not making it. In the end, it was etiquette that decided. It would not be fair to disappear without telling her first. After that, it would be perfectly acceptable. As long as you tell people what you are going to do, he reasoned, it doesn't matter. Then you are free to do what you want.

The number, however, was busy. He waited five minutes and dialed again. Again, the number was busy. For the next hour Quinn alternated between dialing and waiting, always with the same result. At last he called the operator and asked whether the phone was out of order. There would be a charge of thirty cents, he was told. Then came a crackling in the wires, the sound of further dialing, more voices. Quinn tried to imagine what the operators looked like. Then the first woman spoke to him again: the number was busy.

Quinn did not know what to think. There were so many possibilities, he could not even begin. Stillman? The phone off the hook? Someone else altogether?

He turned on the television and watched the first two innings of the Mets game. Then he dialed once again. Same thing. In the top of the third St. Louis scored on a walk, a stolen base, an infield out, and a sacrifice fly. The Mets matched that run in their half of the inning on a double by Wilson and a single by Youngblood. Quinn realized that he didn't care. A beer commercial came on, and he turned off the sound. For the twentieth time he tried to reach Virginia Stillman, and for the twentieth time the same thing happened. In the top of the fourth St. Louis scored five runs, and Quinn turned off the picture as well. He found his red notebook, sat down at his desk, and wrote steadily for the next two hours. He did not bother to read over what he had written. Then he called Virginia Stillman and got another busy signal. He slammed the receiver down so hard that the plastic cracked. When he tried to call again, he could no longer get a dial tone. He stood up, went into the kitchen, and made another bowl of cornflakes. Then he went to bed.

In his dream, which he later forgot, he found himself walking down Broadway, holding Auster's son by the hand.

Quinn spent the following day on his feet. He started early, just after eight o'clock, and did not stop to consider where he was going. As it happened, he saw many things that day he had never noticed before.

Every twenty minutes he would go into a phone booth and call Virginia Stillman. As it had been the night before, so it was today. By now Quinn expected the number to be busy. It no longer even bothered him. The busy signal had become a counterpoint to his steps, a metronome beating steadily inside the random noises of the city. There was comfort in the thought that whenever he dialed the number, the sound would be there for him, never swerving in its denial, negating speech and the possibility of speech, as insistent as the beating of a heart. Virginia and Peter Stillman were shut off from him now. But he could soothe his conscience with the thought that he was still trying. Whatever darkness they were leading him into, he had not abandoned them yet.

He walked down Broadway to 72nd Street, turned east to Central Park West, and followed it to 59th Street and the statue of Columbus. There he turned east once again, moving along Central Park South until Madison Avenue, and then cut right, walking downtown to Grand Central Station. After circling haphazardly for a few blocks, he continued south for a mile, came to the juncture of Broadway and Fifth Avenue at 23rd Street, paused to look at the Flatiron Building, and then shifted course, taking a westward turn until he reached Seventh Avenue, at which point he veered left and progressed further downtown. At Sheridan Square he turned east again, ambling down Waverly Place, crossing Sixth Avenue, and continuing on to Washington Square. He walked through the arch and made his way south among the crowds, stopping momentarily to watch a juggler perform on a slack rope stretched between a light pole and a tree trunk. Then he left the little park at its downtown east corner, went through the university housing project with its patches of green grass, and turned right at Houston Street. At West Broadway he turned again, this time to the left, and proceeded onward to Canal. Angling slightly to this right, he passed through a vest pocket park and swung around to Varick Street, walked by number 6, where he had once lived, and then regained his southern course, picking up West Broadway again where it merged with Varick. West Broadway took him to the base of the World Trade Center and on into the lobby of one of the towers, where he made his thirteenth call of the day to Virginia Stillman. Quinn decided to eat something, entered one of the fast-food places on the ground floor, and leisurely consumed a sandwich as he did some work in the red notebook. Afterwards, he walked east again, wandering through the narrow streets of the financial district, and then headed further south, towards Bowling Green, where he saw the water and the seagulls above it, careening in the midday light. For a moment he considered taking a ride on the Staten Island Ferry, but then thought better of it and began tracking his way to the north. At Fulton Street he slid to his right and followed the northeastward path of East Broadway, which led through the miasma of the Lower East Side and then up into Chinatown. From there he found the Bowery, which carried him along to Fourteenth Street. He then hooked left, cut through Union Square, and continued uptown along Park Avenue South. At 23rd Street he jockeyed north. A few blocks later he jutted right again, went one block to the east, and then walked up Third Avenue for a while. At 32nd Street he turned right, came upon Second Avenue, turned left, moved uptown another three blocks, and then turned right one last time, whereupon he met up with First Avenue. He then walked the remaining seven blocks to the United

Nations and decided to take a short rest. He sat down on a stone bench in the plaza and breathed deeply, idling in the air and the light with closed eyes. Then he opened the red notebook, took the deaf mute's pen from his pocket, and began a new page.

For the first time since he had bought the red notebook, what he wrote that day had nothing to do with the Stillman case. Rather, he concentrated on the things he had seen while walking. He did not stop to think about what he was doing, nor did he analyze the possible implications of this uncustomary act. He felt an urge to record certain facts, and he wanted to put them down on paper before he forgot them.

Today, as never before: the tramps, the down-and-outs, the shopping-bag ladies, the drifters and drunks. They range from the merely destitute to the wretchedly broken. Wherever you turn, they are there, in good neighborhoods and bad.

Some beg with a semblance of pride. Give me this money, they seem to say, and soon I will be back there with the rest of you, rushing back and forth on my daily rounds. Others have given up hope of ever leaving their tramphood. They lie there sprawled out on the sidewalk with their hat, or cup, or box, not even bothering to look up at the passerby, too defeated even to thank the ones who drop a coin beside them. Still others try to work for the money they are given: the blind pencil sellers, the winos who wash the windshield of your car. Some tell stories, usually tragic accounts of their own lives, as if to give their benefactors something for their kindness—even if only words.

Others have real talents. The old black man today, for example, who tap-danced while juggling cigarettes— still dignified, clearly once a vaudevillian, dressed in a purple suit with a green shirt and a yellow tie, his mouth fixed in a half-remembered stage smile. There are also the pavement chalk artists and musicians: saxophonists, electric guitarists, fiddlers. Occasionally, you will even come across a genius, as I did today:

A clarinetist of no particular age, wearing a hat that obscured his face, and sitting cross-legged on the sidewalk, in the manner of a snake-charmer. Directly in front of him were two wind-up monkeys, one with a tambourine and the other with a drum. With the one shaking and the other banging, beating out a weird and precise syncopation, the man would improvise endless tiny variations on his instrument, his body swaying stiffly back and forth, energetically miming the monkeys' rhythm. He played jauntily and with flair, crisp and looping figures in the minor mode, as if glad to be there with his mechanical friends, enclosed in the universe he had created, never once looking up. It went on and on, always finally the same, and yet the longer I listened the harder I found it to leave.

To be inside that music, to be drawn into the circle of its repetitions: perhaps that is a place where one could finally disappear.

But beggars and performers make up only a small part of the vagabond population. They are the aristocracy, the elite of the fallen. Far more numerous are those with nothing to do, with nowhere to go. Many are drunks—but that term does not do justice to the devastation they embody. Hulks of despair, clothed in rags, their faces bruised and bleeding, they shuffle through the streets as though in chains. Asleep in doorways, staggering insanely through traffic, collapsing on sidewalks—they seem to be everywhere the moment you look for them. Some will starve to death, others will die of exposure, still others will be beaten or burned or tortured.

For every soul lost in this particular hell, there are several others locked inside madness—unable to exit to the world that stands at the threshold of their bodies. Even though they seem to be there, they cannot be counted as present. The man, for example, who goes everywhere with a set of drumsticks, pounding the pavement with them in a reckless, nonsensical rhythm, stooped over awkwardly as he advances along the street, beating and beating away at the cement. Perhaps he thinks he is doing important work. Perhaps, if he did not do what he did, the city would fall apart. Perhaps the moon would spin out of its orbit and come crashing into the earth. There are the ones who talk to themselves, who mutter, who scream, who curse, who groan, who tell themselves stories as if to someone else. The man I saw today, sitting like a heap of garbage in front of Grand Central Station, the crowds rushing past him, saying in a loud, panic-stricken voice: "Third Marines. . . .Eating bees. . . .The bees crawling out of my mouth." Or the woman shouting at an invisible companion: "And what if I don't want to! What if I just fucking don't want to!"

There are the women with their shopping bags and the men with their cardboard boxes, hauling their possessions from one place to the next, forever on the move, as if it mattered where they were. There is the man wrapped in the American flag. There is the woman with a Halloween mask on her face. There is the man in a ravaged overcoat, his shoes wrapped in rags, carrying a perfectly pressed white shirt on a hanger—still sheathed in the dry-cleaner's plastic. There is the man in a business suit with bare feet and a football helmet on his head. There is the woman whose clothes are covered from head to toe with Presidential campaign buttons. There is the man who walks with his face in his hands, weeping hysterically and saying over and over again: "No, no, no. He's dead. He's not dead. No, no, no. He's dead. He's not dead."

Baudelaire: Il me semble que je serais toujours bien là où je ne suis pas. In other words: It seems to me that I will always be happy in the place where I am not. Or, more bluntly: Wherever I am not is the place where I am myself. Or else, taking the bull by the horns: Anywhere out of the world.

It was almost evening. Quinn closed the red notebook and put the pen in his pocket. He wanted to think a little more about what he had written but found he could not. The air around him was soft, almost sweet, as though it no longer belonged to the city. He stood up from the bench, stretched his arms and legs, and walked to a phone booth, where he called Virginia Stillman again. Then he went to dinner.

In the restaurant he realized that he had come to a decision about things. Without his even knowing it, the answer was already there for him, sitting fully formed in his head. The busy signal, he saw now, had not been arbitrary. It had been a sign, and it was telling him that he could not yet break his connection with the case, even if he wanted to. He had tried to contact Virginia Stillman in order to tell her that he was through, but the fates had not allowed it. Quinn paused to consider this. Was "fate" really the word he wanted to use? It seemed like such a ponderous and old-fashioned choice. And yet, as he probed more deeply into it, he discovered that was precisely what he meant to say. Or, if not precisely, it came closer than any other term he could think of. Fate in the sense of what was, of what happened to be. It was something like the word "it" in the phrase "it is raining" or "it is night." What that "it" referred to Quinn had never known. A generalized condition of things as they were, perhaps; the state of is-ness that was the ground on which the happenings of the world took place. He could not be any more definite than that. But perhaps he was not really searching for anything definite.

It was fate, then. Whatever he thought of it, however much he might want it to be different, there was nothing he could do about it. He had said yes to a proposition, and now he was powerless to undo that yes. That meant only one thing: he had to go through with it. There could not be two answers. It was either this or that. And so it was, whether he liked it or not.

The business about Auster was clearly a mistake. Perhaps there had once been a private detective in New York with that name. The husband of Peter's nurse was a retired policeman—therefore not a young man. In his day there had no doubt been an Auster with a good reputation, and he had naturally thought of him when called upon to provide a detective. He had looked in the telephone book, had found only one person with that name and assumed he had the right man. Then he gave the number to the Stillmans. At that point, the second mistake had occurred. There had been a foul-up in the lines, and somehow his number had got crossed with Auster's. That kind of thing happened every day. And so he had received the call— which anyway had been destined for the wrong man. It all made perfect sense.

One problem still remained. If he was unable to contact Virginia Stillman—if, as he believed, he was meant *not* to contact her—how exactly was he to proceed? His job was to protect Peter, to make sure that no harm came to him. Did it matter what Virginia Stillman thought he was doing as long as he did what he was supposed to do? Ideally, an operative should maintain close contact with his client. That had always been one of Max Work's principles. But was it really necessary? As long as Quinn did his job, how could it matter? If there were any misunderstandings, surely they could be cleared up once the case was settled.

He could proceed, then, as he wished. He would no longer have to telephone Virginia Stillman. He could abandon the oracular busy signal once and for all. From now on, there would be no stopping him. It would be impossible for Stillman to come near Peter without Quinn knowing about it.

Quinn paid up his check, put a mentholated toothpick in his mouth, and began walking again. He did not have far to go. Along the way, he stopped at a twenty-four-hour Citibank and checked his balance with the automatic teller. There were three hundred and forty-nine dollars in his account. He withdrew three hundred, put the cash in his pocket, and continued uptown. At 57th Street he turned left and walked to Park Avenue. There he turned right and went on walking north until 69th Street, at which point he turned onto the Stillmans' block. The building looked the same as it had on the first day. He glanced up to see if there were any lights on in the apartment, but he could not remember which windows were theirs. The street was utterly quiet. No cars drove down it, no people passed. Quinn stepped across to the other side, found a spot for himself in a narrow alleyway, and settled in for the night.

12

A long time passed. Exactly how long it is impossible to say. Weeks certainly, but perhaps even months. The acccount of this period is less full than the author would have liked. But information is scarce, and he has preferred to pass over in silence what could not be definitely confirmed. Since this story is based entirely on facts, the author feels it his duty not to overstep the bounds of the verifiable, to resist at all costs the perils of invention. Even the red notebook, which until now has provided a detailed account of Quinn's experiences, is suspect. We cannot say for certain what happened to Quinn during this period, for it is at this point in the story that he began to lose his grip.

He remained for the most part in the alley. It was not uncomfortable once he got used to it, and it had the advantage of being well hidden from view. From there he could observe all the comings and goings at the Stillmans' building. No one left and no one entered without his seeing who it was. In the beginning, it surprised him that he saw neither Virginia nor Peter. But there were many delivery

men constantly coming and going, and eventually he realized that it was not necessary for them to leave the building. Everything could be brought to them. It was then that
Quinn understood that they, too, were holing up, waiting
inside their apartment for the case to end.

Little by little, Quinn adapted to his new life. There
were a number of problems to be faced, but one by one
he managed to solve them. First of all, there was the
question of food. Because utmost vigilance was required
of him, he was reluctant to leave his post for any length
of time. It tormented him to think that something might
happen in his absence, and he made every effort to min-
imize the risks. He had read somewhere that between 3:30
and 4:30 A.M. there were more people asleep in their beds
than at any other time. Statistically speaking, the chances
were best that nothing would happen during that hour, and
therefore Quinn chose it as the time to do his shopping.
On Lexington Avenue not far north there was an all-night
grocery, and at three-thirty every morning Quinn would
walk there at a brisk pace (for the exercise, and also to
save time) and buy whatever he needed for the next twenty-
four hours. It turned out not to be much—and, as it happened, he needed less and less as time went on. For Quinn
learned that eating did not necessarily solve the problem
of food. A meal was no more than a fragile defense against
the inevitability of the next meal. Food itself could never
answer the question of food; it only delayed the moment

when the question would have to be asked in earnest. The greatest danger, therefore, was in eating too much. If he took in more than he should, his appetite for the next meal increased, and thus more food was needed to satisfy him. By keeping a close and constant watch on himself, Quinn was gradually able to reverse the process. His ambition was to eat as little as possible, and in this way to stave off his hunger. In the best of all worlds, he might have been able to approach absolute zero, but he did not want to be overly ambitious in his present circumstances. Rather, he kept the total fast in his mind as an ideal, a state of perfection he could aspire to but never achieve. He did not want to starve himself to death—and he reminded himself of this every day—he simply wanted to leave himself free to think of the things that truly concerned him. For now, that meant keeping the case uppermost in his thoughts. Fortunately, this coincided with his other major ambition: to make the three hundred dollars last as long as he could. It goes without saying that Quinn lost a good deal of weight during this period.

His second problem was sleep. He could not stay awake all the time, and yet that was really what the situation required. Here, too, he was forced to make certain concessions. As with eating, Quinn felt that he could make do with less than he was accustomed to. Instead of the six to eight hours of sleep he was used to getting, he decided to limit himself to three or four. Adjusting to this was difficult, but far more difficult was the problem of how to distribute these hours so as to maintain maximum vigilance. Clearly, he could not sleep for three or four hours in a row. The risks were simply too great. Theoretically, the most efficient use of the time would be to sleep for thirty seconds every five or six minutes. That would reduce his chances of missing something almost to nil. But he realized that this was physically impossible. On the other hand, using this impossibility as a kind of model, he tried to train himself into taking a series of short naps, alternating between sleeping and waking as often as he could. It was a long struggle, demanding discipline and concentration, for the longer the experiment went on, the more exhausted he became. In the beginning, he tried for sequences of forty-five minutes each, then gradually reduced them to thirty minutes. Towards the end, he had begun to manage the fifteen-minute nap with a fair amount of success. He was helped in his efforts by a nearby church, whose bells rang every fifteen minutes—one stroke on the quarter-hour, two strokes on the half-hour, three strokes on the three-quarter-hour, and four strokes on the hour, followed by the appropriate number of strokes for the hour itself. Quinn lived by the rhythm of that clock, and eventually he had trouble distinguishing it from his own pulse. Starting at midnight, he would begin his routine, closing his eyes and falling asleep before the clock had struck twelve. Fifteen minutes later he would wake, at the half-hour double stroke fall asleep, and at the three-quarter-hour triple stroke wake once more. At three-thirty he would go off for his food, return by four o'clock, and then go to sleep again. His dreams during this period were few. When they did occur, they were strange: brief visions of the immediate—his hands, his shoes, the brick wall beside him. Nor was there ever a moment when he was not dead tired.

His third problem was shelter, but this was more easily solved than the other two. Fortunately, the weather remained warm, and as late spring moved into summer, there was little rain. Every now and then there was a shower, and once or twice a downpour with thunder and lightning, but all in all it was not bad, and Quinn never stopped giving thanks for his luck. At the back of the alley there was a large metal bin for garbage, and whenever it rained at night Quinn would climb into it for protection. Inside, the smell was overpowering, and it would permeate his clothes for days on end, but Quinn preferred it to getting wet, for he did not want to run the risk of catching cold or falling ill. Happily, the lid had been bent out of shape and did not fit tightly over the bin. In one corner there was a gap of six or eight inches that formed a kind of air hole for Quinn to breathe through—sticking his nose out into the night. By standing on his knees on top of the garbage and leaning his body against one wall of the bin, he found that he was not altogether uncomfortable.

On clear nights he would sleep under the bin, positioning his head in such a way that the moment he opened his eyes he could see the front door of Stillmans' building. As for emptying his bladder, he usually did this in the far corner of the alley, behind the bin and with his back to the street. His bowels were another matter, and for this he would climb into the bin to ensure privacy. There were also a number of plastic garbage cans beside the bin, and from one of these Quinn was usually able to find a sufficiently clean newspaper to wipe himself, although once, in an emergency, he was forced to use a page from the red notebook. As for washing and shaving, these were two of the things that Quinn learned to live without.

How he managed to keep himself hidden during this period is a mystery. But it seems that no one discovered him or called his presence to the attention of the authorities. No doubt he learned early on the schedule of the garbage collectors and made sure to be out of the alley when they came. Likewise the building superintendent, who deposited the trash each evening in the bin and the cans. Remarkable as it seems, no one ever noticed Quinn. It was as though he had melted into the walls of the city.

The problems of housekeeping and material life occupied a certain portion of each day. For the most part, however, Quinn had time on his hands. Because he did not want anyone to see him, he had to avoid other people as systematically as he could. He could not look at them, he could not talk to them, he could not think about them.

Quinn had always thought of himself as a man who liked to be alone. For the past five years, in fact, he had actively sought it. But it was only now, as his life continued in the alley, that he began to understand the true nature of solitude. He had nothing to fall back on anymore but himself. And of all the things he discovered during the days he was there, this was the one he did not doubt: that he was falling. What he did not understand, however, was this: in that he was falling, how could he be expected to catch himself as well? Was it possible to be at the top and the bottom at the same time? It did not seem to make sense.

He spent many hours looking up at the sky. From his position at the back of the alley, wedged in between the bin and the wall, there were few other things to see, and as the days passed he began to take pleasure in the world overhead. He saw that, above all, the sky was never still. Even on cloudless days, when the blue seemed to be everywhere, there were constant little shifts, gradual disturbances as the sky thinned out and grew thick, the sudden whitenesses of planes, birds, and flying papers. Clouds complicated the picture, and Quinn spent many afternoons studying them, trying to learn their ways, seeing if he could not predict what would happen to them. He became familiar with the cirrus, the cumulus, the stratus, the nimbus, and all their various combinations, watching for each one in its turn, and seeing how the sky would change under its influence. Clouds, too, introduced the matter of color, and there was a wide range to contend with, spanning from black to white, with an infinity of grays between. These all had to be investigated, measured, and deciphered. On top of this, there were the pastels that formed whenever the sun and the clouds interacted at certain times of day. The spectrum of variables was immense, the result depending on the temperatures of the different atmosphere levels, the types of clouds present in the sky, and where the sun happened to be at that particular moment. From all this came the reds and pinks that Quinn liked so much, the purples and vermilions, the oranges and lavenders, the golds and feathery persimmons. Nothing lasted for long. The colors would soon disperse, merging with others and moving on or fading as the night appeared. Almost always there was a wind to hasten these events. From where he sat in the alley, Quinn could rarely feel it, but by watching its effect on the clouds, he could gauge its intensity and the nature of the air it carried. One by one, all weathers passed over his head, from sunshine to storms, from gloom to radiance. There were the dawns and dusks to observe, the midday transformations, the early evenings, the nights. Even in its blackness, the sky did not rest. Clouds drifted through the dark, the moon was forever in a different form, the wind continued to blow. Sometimes a star even settled into Quinn's patch of sky, and as he looked up he would wonder if it was still there, or if it had not burned out long ago.

●

The days therefore came and went. Stillman did not appear. Quinn's money ran out at last. For some time he had been steeling himself for this moment, and towards the end he hoarded his funds with maniacal precision. No penny was spent without first judging the necessity of what he thought he needed, without first weighing all the consequences, pro and con. But not even the most stringent economies could halt the march of the inevitable.

It was some time in mid-August when Quinn discovered that he no longer could hold out. The author has confirmed this date through diligent research. It is possible, however, that this moment occurred as early as late July, or as late as early September, since all investigations of this sort must make allowances for a certain margin of error. But, to the best of his knowledge, having considered the evidence carefully and sifted through all apparent contradictions, the author places the following events in August, somewhere between the twelfth and twenty-fifth of the month.

Quinn had almost nothing now—a few coins that amounted to less than a dollar. He was certain that money had arrived for him during his absence. It was simply a matter of retrieving the checks from his mailbox at the post office, taking them to the bank, and cashing them. If all went well, he could be back to East 69th Street within a few hours. We will never know the agonies he suffered at having to leave his spot.

He did not have enough money to take the bus. For the

first time in many weeks, then, he began to walk. It was odd to be on his feet again, moving steadily from one place to the next, swinging his arms back and forth, feeling the pavement under the soles of his shoes. And yet there he was, walking west on 69th Street, turning right on Madison Avenue, and beginning to make his way north. His legs were weak, and he felt as though his head were made of air. He had to stop every now and then to catch his breath, and once, on the brink of falling, he had to grab hold of a lamp post. He found that things went better if he lifted his feet as little as possible, shuffling forward with slow, sliding steps. In this way he could conserve his strength for the corners, where he had to balance himself carefully before and after each step up and down from the curb.

At 84th Street he paused momentarily in front of a shop. There was a mirror on the facade, and for the first time since he had begun his vigil, Quinn saw himself. It was not that he had been afraid to confront his own image. Quite simply, it had not occurred to him. He had been too busy with his job to think about himself, and it was as though the question of his appearance had ceased to exist. Now, as he looked at himself in the shop mirror, he was neither shocked nor disappointed. He had no feeling about it at all, for the fact was that he did not recognize the person he saw there as himself. He thought that he had spotted a stranger in the mirror, and in that first moment he turned around sharply to see who it was. But there was no one near him. Then he turned back to examine the mirror more carefully. Feature by feature, he studied the face in front of him and slowly began to notice that this person bore a certain resemblance to the man he had always thought of as himself. Yes, it seemed more than likely that this was Quinn. Even now, however, he was not upset. The transformation in his appearance had been so drastic that he could not help but be fascinated by it. He had turned into a bum. His clothes were discolored, disheveled, debauched by filth. His face was covered by a thick black beard with tiny flecks of gray in it. His hair was long and tangled, matted into tufts behind his ears, and crawling down in curls almost to his shoulders. More than anything else, he reminded himself of Robinson Crusoe, and he marveled at how quickly these changes had taken place in him. It had been no more than a matter of months, and in that time he had become someone else. He tried to remember himself as he had been before, but he found it difficult. He looked at this new Quinn and shrugged. It did not really matter. He had been one thing before, and now he was another. It was neither better nor worse. It was different, and that was all.

He continued uptown for several more blocks, then turned left, crossed Fifth Avenue, and walked along the wall of Central Park. At 96th Street he entered the park and found himself glad to be among the grass and trees. Late summer had exhausted much of the greenness, and here and there the ground showed through in brown, dusty patches. But the trees overhead were still filled with leaves, and everywhere there was a sparkling of light and shade that struck Quinn as miraculous and beautiful. It was late morning, and the heavy heat of the afternoon lay several hours off.

Halfway through the park Quinn was overtaken by an urge to rest. There were no streets here, no city blocks to mark the stages of his progress, and it seemed to him suddenly that he had been walking for hours. Making it to the other side of the park felt as though it would take another day or two of dogged hiking. He went on for a few more minutes, but at last his legs gave out. There was an oak tree not far from where he stood, and Quinn went for it now, staggering in the way a drunk gropes for his bed after an all-night binge. Using the red notebook as a pillow, he lay down on a grassy mound just north of the tree and fell asleep. It was the first unbroken sleep he had had in months, and he did not wake until it was morning again.

His watch said that it was nine-thirty, and he cringed to think of the time he had lost. Quinn stood up and began loping towards the west, amazed that his strength was back, but cursing himself for the hours he had wasted in getting it. He was beyond consolation. No matter what he did now, he felt that he would always be too late. He could run for a hundred years, and still he would arrive just as the doors were closing.

He emerged from the park at 96th Street and continued west. At the corner of Columbus Avenue he saw a telephone booth, which suddenly reminded him of Auster and the five-hundred-dollar check. Perhaps he could save time by collecting the money now. He could go directly to Auster, put the cash in his pocket, and avoid the trip to the post office and the bank. But would Auster have the cash on hand? If not, perhaps they could arrange to meet at Auster's bank.

Quinn entered the booth, dug into his pocket, and removed what money was left: two dimes, a quarter, and eight pennies. He dialed information for the number, got his dime back in the coin return box, deposited the dime again, and dialed. Auster picked up on the third ring.

"Quinn here," said Quinn.

He heard a groan on the other end. "Where the hell have you been hiding?" There was irritation in Auster's voice. "I've called you a thousand times."

"I've been busy. Working on the case."

"The case?"

"The case. The Stillman case. Remember?"

"Of course I remember."

"That's why I'm calling. I want to come for the money now. The five hundred dollars."

"What money?"

"The check, remember? The check I gave you. The one made out to Paul Auster."

"Of course I remember. But there is no money. That's why I've been trying to call you."

"You had no right to spend it," Quinn shouted, suddenly beside himself. "That money belonged to me."

"I didn't spend it. The check bounced."

"I don't believe you."

"You can come here and see the letter from the bank, if you want. It's sitting here on my desk. The check was no good."

"That's absurd."

"Yes, it is. But it hardly matters now, does it?"

"Of course it matters. I need the money to go on with the case."

"But there is no case. It's all over."

"What are you talking about?"

"The same thing you are. The Stillman case."

"But what do you mean 'it's over?' I'm still working on it."

"I can't believe it."

"Stop being so goddamn mysterious. I don't have the slightest idea what you're talking about."

"I don't believe you don't know. Where the hell have you been? Don't you read the newspapers?"

"Newspapers? Goddamit, say what you mean. I don't have time to read newspapers."

There was a silence on the other end, and for a moment Quinn felt that the conversation was over, that he had somehow fallen asleep and had just now woken up to find the telephone in his hand.

"Stillman jumped off the Brooklyn Bridge, " Auster said. "He committed suicide two and a half months ago."

"You're lying."

"It was all over the papers. You can check for yourself."

Quinn said nothing.

"It was your Stillman," Auster went on. "The one who used to be a Professor at Columbia. They say he died in mid-air, before he even hit the water."

"And Peter? What about Peter?"

"I have no idea."

"Does anybody know?"

"Impossible to say. You'd have to find that out yourself."

"Yes, I suppose so," said Quinn.

Then, without saying good-bye to Auster, he hung up. He took the other dime and used it to call Virginia Stillman. He still knew the number by heart.

A mechanical voice spoke the number back to him and announced that it had been disconnected. The voice then repeated the message, and afterwards the line went dead.

Quinn could not be sure what he felt. In those first moments, it was as though he felt nothing, as though the whole thing added up to nothing at all. He decided to postpone thinking about it. There would be time for that later, he thought. For now, the only thing that seemed to matter was going home. He would return to his apartment, take off his clothes, and sit in a hot bath. Then he would look through the new magazines, play a few records, do a little housecleaning. Then, perhaps, he would begin to think about it.

He walked back to 107th Street. The keys to his house were still in his pocket, and as he unlocked his front door and walked up the three flights to his apartment, he felt almost happy. But then he stepped into the apartment, and that was the end of that.

Everything had changed. It seemed like another place altogether, and Quinn thought he must have entered the wrong apartment by mistake. He backed into the hall and checked the number on the door. No, he had not been wrong. It was his apartment; it was his key that had opened the door. He walked back inside and took stock of the situation. The furniture had been rearranged. Where there had once been a table there was now a chair. Where there had once been a sofa there was now a table. There were new pictures on the walls, a new rug was on the floor. And his desk? He looked for it but could not find it. He studied the furniture more carefully and saw that it was not his. What had been there the last time he was in the apartment had been removed. His desk was gone, his books were gone, the child drawings of his dead son were gone. He went from the living room to the bedroom. His bed was gone, his bureau was gone. He opened the top drawer of

the bureau that was there. Women's underthings lay tangled in random clumps: panties, bras, slips. The next
drawer held women's sweaters. Quinn went no further than
that. On a table near the bed there was a framed photograph
of a blond, beefy-faced young man. Another photograph
showed the same young man smiling, standing in the snow
with his arm around an insipid-looking girl. She, too, was
smiling. Behind them there was a ski slope, a man with
two skis on his shoulder, and the blue winter sky.

Quinn went back to the living room and sat down in a
chair. He saw a half-smoked cigarette with lipstick on it
in an ashtray. He lit it up and smoked it. Then he went
into the kitchen, opened the refrigerator, and found some
orange juice and a loaf of bread. He drank the juice, ate
three slices of bread, and then returned to the living room,
where he sat down in the chair again. Fifteen minutes later
he heard footsteps coming up the stairs, a jangling of keys
outside the door, and then the girl from the photograph
entered the apartment. She was wearing a white nurse's
uniform and held a brown grocery bag in her arms. When
she saw Quinn, she dropped the bag and screamed. Or
else she screamed first and then dropped the bag. Quinn
could never be sure which. The bag ripped open when it
hit the floor, and milk gurgled in a white path toward the
edge of the rug.

Quinn stood up, raised his hand in a gesture of peace,
and told her not to worry. He wasn't going to hurt her.

The only thing he wanted to know was why she was living in his apartment. He took the key from his pocket and held it up in the air, as if to prove his good intentions. It took him a while to convince her, but at last her panic subsided.

That did not mean she had begun to trust him or that she was any less afraid. She hung by the open door, ready to make a dash for it at the first sign of trouble. Quinn held his distance, not wanting to make things worse. His mouth kept talking, explaining again and again that she was living in his house. She clearly did not believe one word of it, but she listened in order to humor him, no doubt hoping that he would talk himself out and finally leave.

"I've been living here for a month," she said. "It's my apartment. I signed a year's lease."

"But why do I have the key?" Quinn asked for the seventh or eighth time. "Doesn't that convince you?"

"There are hundred of ways you could have got that key."

"Didn't they tell you there was someone living here when you rented the place?"

"They said it was a writer. But he disappeared, hadn't paid his rent in months."

"That's me!" shouted Quinn. "I'm the writer!"

The girl looked him over coldly and laughed. "A writer? That's the funniest thing I ever heard. Just look at you. I've never seen a bigger mess in all my life."

"I've had some difficulties lately," muttered Quinn, by way of explanation. "But it's only temporary."

"The landlord told me he was glad to get rid of you anyway. He doesn't like tenants who don't have jobs. They use too much heat and run down the fixtures."

"Do you know what happened to my things?"

"What things?"

"My books. My furniture. My papers."

"I have no idea. They probably sold what they could and threw the rest away. Everything was cleared out before I moved in."

Quinn let out a deep sigh. He had come to the end of himself. He could feel it now, as though a great truth had finally dawned in him. There was nothing left.

"Do you realize what this means?" he asked.

"Frankly, I don't care," the girl said. "It's your problem, not mine. I just want you to get out of here. Right now. This is my place, and I want you out. If you don't leave, I'm going to call the police and have you arrested."

It didn't matter anymore. He could stand there arguing with the girl for the rest of the day, and still he wouldn't get his apartment back. It was gone, he was gone, everything was gone. He stammered something inaudible, excused himself for taking up her time, and walked past her out the door.

13

BECAUSE it no longer mattered to him what happened, Quinn was not surprised that the front door at 69th Street opened without a key. Nor was he surprised when he reached the ninth floor and walked down the corridor to the Stillmans' apartment that that door should be open as well. Least of all did it surprise him to find the apartment empty. The place had been stripped bare, and the rooms now held nothing. Each one was identical to every other: a wooden floor and four white walls. This made no particular impression on Quinn. He was exhausted, and the only thing he could think of was closing his eyes.

He went to one of the rooms at the back of the apartment, a small space that measured no more than ten feet by six feet. It had one wire-mesh window that gave on to a view of the airshaft, and of all the rooms it seemed to be the darkest. Within this room there was a second door which led to a windowless cubicle that contained a toilet and a sink. Quinn put the red notebook on the floor, removed the deaf mute's pen from his pocket, and tossed it onto the red notebook. Then he took off his watch and put it in his pocket. After that he took off all his clothes, opened the window, and one by one dropped each thing down the airshaft: first his right shoe, then his left shoe; one sock, then the other sock; his shirt, his jacket, his underpants, his pants. He did not look out to watch them fall, nor did he check to see where they landed. Then he closed the window, lay down in the center of the floor, and went to sleep.

It was dark in the room when he woke up. Quinn could not be sure how much time had passed—whether it was the night of that day or the night of the next. It was even possible, he thought, that it was not night at all. Perhaps it was merely dark inside the room, and outside, beyond the window, the sun was shining. For several moments he considered getting up and going to the window to see, but then he decided it did not matter. If it was not night now, he thought, then night would come later. That was certain, and whether he looked out the window or not, the answer would be the same. On the other hand, if it was in fact night here in New York, then surely the sun was shining somewhere else. In China, for example, it was no doubt mid-afternoon, and the rice farmers were mopping sweat from their brows. Night and day were no more than relative terms; they did not refer to an absolute condition. At any given moment, it was always both. The only reason we did not know it was because we could not be in two places at the same time.

Quinn also considered getting up and going to another room, but then he realized that he was quite happy where he was. It was comfortable here in the spot he had chosen, and he found that he enjoyed lying on his back with his eyes open, looking up at the ceiling—or what would have been the ceiling, had he been able to see it. Only one thing was lacking for him, and that was the sky. He realized that he missed having it overhead, after so many days and nights spent in the open. But he was inside now, and no matter what room he chose to camp in, the sky would remain hidden, inaccessible even at the farthest limit of sight.

He thought he would stay there until he no longer could. There would be water from the sink to quench his thirst, and that would buy him some time. Eventually, he would get hungry and have to eat. But he had been working for so long now at wanting so little that he knew this moment was still several days off. He decided not to think about it until he had to. There was no sense in worrying, he thought, no sense in troubling himself with things that did not matter.

He tried to think about the life he had lived before the story began. This caused many difficulties, for it seemed so remote to him now. He remembered the books he had written under the name of William Wilson. It was strange, he thought, that he had done that, and he wondered now why he had. In his heart, he realized that Max Work was dead. He had died somewhere on the way to his next case, and Quinn could not bring himself to feel sorry. It all seemed so unimportant now. He thought back to his desk and the thousands of words he had written there. He thought back to the man who had been his agent and realized he could not remember his name. So many things were disappearing now, it was difficult to keep track of them. Quinn tried to work his way through the Mets' lineup, position by position, but his mind was beginning to wander. The centerfielder, he remembered, was Mookie Wilson, a promising young player whose real name was William Wilson. Surely there was something interesting in that. Quinn pursued the idea for a few moments but then abandoned it. The two William Wilsons cancelled each other out, and that was all. Quinn waved good-bye to them in his mind. The Mets would finish in last place again, and no one would suffer.

The next time he woke up, the sun was shining in the room. There was a tray of food beside him on the floor, the dishes steaming with what looked like a roast beef dinner. Quinn accepted this fact without protest. He was neither surprised nor disturbed by it. Yes, he said to himself, it is perfectly possible that food should have been left here for me. He was not curious to know how or why this had taken place. It did not even occur to him to leave the room to look through the rest of the apartment for an answer. Rather, he examined the food on the tray more closely and saw that in addition to two large slices of roast beef there were seven little roast potatoes, a plate of asparagus, a fresh roll, a salad, a carafe of red wine, and wedges of cheese and a pear for dessert. There was a white linen napkin, and the silverware was of the finest quality. Quinn ate the food—or half of it, which was as much as he could manage.

After his meal, he began to write in the red notebook. He continued writing until darkness returned to the room. There was a small light fixture in the middle of the ceiling and a switch for it by the door, but the thought of using it did not appeal to Quinn. Not long after that he fell asleep again. When he woke up, there was sunlight in the room and another tray of food beside him on the floor. He ate what he could of the food and then went back to writing in the red notebook.

For the most part his entries from this period consisted of marginal questions concerning the Stillman case. Quinn wondered, for example, why he had not bothered to look up the newspaper reports of Stillman's arrest in 1969. He examined the problem of whether the moon landing of that same year had been connected in any way with what had happened. He asked himself why he had taken Auster's word for it that Stillman was dead. He tried to think about eggs and wrote out such phrases as "a good egg," "egg on his face," "to lay an egg," "to be as like as two eggs." He wondered what would have happened if he had followed the second Stillman instead of the first. He asked himself why Christopher, the patron saint of travel, had been decanonized by the Pope in 1969, just at the time of the trip to the moon. He thought through the question of why Don Quixote had not simply wanted to write books like the ones he loved—instead of living out their adventures. He wondered why he had the same initials as Don Quixote. He considered whether the girl who had moved into his apartment was the same girl he had seen in Grand Central Station reading his book. He wondered if Virginia Stillman had hired another detective after he failed to get in touch with her. He asked himself why he had taken Auster's word for it that the check had bounced. He thought about Peter Stillman and wondered if he had ever slept in the room he was in now. He wondered if the case was really over or if he was not somehow still working on it. He wondered what the map would look like of all the steps he had taken in his life and what word it would spell.

When it was dark, Quinn slept, and when it was light he ate the food and wrote in the red notebook. He could never be sure how much time passed during each interval, for he did not concern himself with counting the days or the hours. It seemed to him, however, that little by little the darkness had begun to win out over the light, that whereas in the beginning there had been a predominance of sunshine, the light had gradually become fainter and more fleeting. At first, he attributed this to a change of season. The equinox had surely passed already, and perhaps the solstice was approaching. But even after winter had come and the process should theoretically have started to reverse itself, Quinn observed that the periods of dark nevertheless kept gaining on the periods of light. It seemed to him that he had less and less time to eat his food and write in the red notebook. Eventually, it seemed to him that these periods had been reduced to a matter of minutes. Once, for example, he finished his food and discovered that there was only enough time to write three sentences in the red notebook. The next time there was light, he could only manage two sentences. He began to skip his meals in order to devote himself to the red notebook, eating only when he felt he could no longer hold out. But the time continued to diminish, and soon he was able to eat no more than a bite or two before the darkness came back. He did not think of turning on the electric light, for he had long ago forgotten it was there.

This period of growing darkness coincided with the dwindling of pages in the red notebook. Little by little, Quinn was coming to the end. At a certain point, he realized that the more he wrote, the sooner the time would come when he could no longer write anything. He began to weigh his words with great care, struggling to express himself as economically and clearly as possible. He regretted having wasted so many pages at the beginning of the red notebook, and in fact felt sorry that he had bothered to write about the Stillman case at all. For the case was far behind him now, and he no longer bothered to think about it. It had been a bridge to another place in his life, and now that he had crossed it, its meaning had been lost. Quinn no longer had any interest in himself. He wrote about the stars, the earth, his hopes for mankind. He felt that his words had been severed from him, that now they were a part of the world at large, as real and specific as a stone, or a lake, or a flower. They no longer had anything to do with him. He remembered the moment of his birth and how he had been pulled gently from his mother's womb. He remembered the infinite kindnesses of the world and all the people he had ever loved. Nothing mattered now but the beauty of all this. He wanted to go on writing about it, and it pained him to know that this would not be possible. Nevertheless, he tried to face the end of the red notebook with courage. He wondered if he had it in him to write without a pen, if he could learn to speak instead, filling the darkness with his voice, speaking the words into the air, into the walls, into the city, even if the light never came back again.

The last sentence of the red notebook reads: "What will happen when there are no more pages in the red notebook?"

At this point the story grows obscure. The information has run out, and the events that follow this last sentence will never be known. It would be foolish even to hazard a guess.

I returned home from my trip to Africa in February, just hours before a snowstorm began to fall on New York. I called my friend Auster that evening, and he urged me to come over to see him as soon as I could. There was something so insistent in his voice that I dared not refuse, even though I was exhausted.

At his apartment, Auster explained to me what little he knew about Quinn, and then he went on to describe the strange case he had accidentally become involved in. He had become obsessed by it, he said, and he wanted my advice about what he should do. Having heard him out, I began to feel angry that he had treated Quinn with such indifference. I scolded him for not having taken a greater part in events, for not having done something to help a man who was so obviously in trouble.

Auster seemed to take my words to heart. In fact, he said, that was why he had asked me over. He had been feeling guilty and needed to unburden himself. He said that I was the only person he could trust.

He had spent the last several months trying to track down Quinn, but with no success. Quinn was no longer living in his apartment, and all attempts to reach Virginia Stillman had failed. It was then that I suggested that we take a look at the Stillman apartment. Somehow, I had an intuition that this was where Quinn had wound up.

We put on our coats, went outside, and took a cab to East 69th Street. The snow had been falling for an hour, and already the roads were treacherous. We had little trouble getting into the building—slipping through the door with one of the tenants who was just coming home. We went upstairs and found the door to what had once been the Stillmans' apartment. It was unlocked. We stepped in cautiously and discovered a series of bare, empty rooms. In a small room at the back, impeccably clean as all the other rooms were, the red notebook was lying on the floor. Auster picked it up, looked through it briefly, and said that it was Quinn's. Then he handed it to me and said that I should keep it. The whole business had upset him so much that he was afraid to keep it himself. I said that I would hold on to it until he was ready to read it, but he shook his head and told me that he never wanted to see it again. Then we left and walked out into the snow. The city was entirely white now, and the snow kept falling, as though it would never end.

As for Quinn, it is impossible for me to say where he is now. I have followed the red notebook as closely as I could, and any inaccuracies in the story should be blamed on me. There were moments when the text was difficult to decipher, but I have done my best with it and have re-frained from any interpretation. The red notebook, of course, is only half the story, as any sensitive reader will under-stand. As for Auster, I am convinced that he behaved badly throughout. If our friendship has ended, he has only himself to blame. As for me, my thoughts remain with Quinn. He will be with me always. And wherever he may have disappeared to, I wish him luck.

FOR THE BEST IN PAPERBACKS, LOOK FOR THE

In every corner of the world, on every subject under the sun, Penguin represents quality and variety—the very best in publishing today.

For complete information about books available from Penguin—including Pelicans, Puffins, Peregrines, and Penguin Classics—and how to order them, write to us at the appropriate address below. Please note that for copyright reasons the selection of books varies from country to country.

In the United Kingdom: For a complete list of books available from Penguin in the U.K., please write to *Dept E.P., Penguin Books Ltd, Harmondsworth, Middlesex, UB7 0DA.*

In the United States: For a complete list of books available from Penguin in the U.S., please write to *Dept BA, Penguin*, Box 120, Bergenfield, New Jersey 07621-0120.,

In Canada: For a complete list of books available from Penguin in Canada, please write to *Penguin Books Ltd, 2801 John Street, Markham, Ontario L3R 1B4.*

In Australia: For a complete list of books available from Penguin in Australia, please write to the *Marketing Department, Penguin Books Ltd, P.O. Box 257, Ringwood, Victoria 3134.*

In New Zealand: For a complete list of books available from Penguin in New Zealand, please write to the *Marketing Department, Penguin Books (NZ) Ltd, Private Bag, Takapuna, Auckland 9.*

In India: For a complete list of books available from Penguin, please write to *Penguin Overseas Ltd, 706 Eros Apartments, 56 Nehru Place, New Delhi, 110019.*

In Holland: For a complete list of books available from Penguin in Holland, please write to *Penguin Books Nederland B.V., Postbus 195, NL-1380AD Weesp, Netherlands.*

In Germany: For a complete list of books available from Penguin, please write to *Penguin Books Ltd, Friedrichstrasse 10-12, D-6000 Frankfurt Main 1, Federal Republic of Germany.*

In Spain: For a complete list of books available from Penguin in Spain, please write to *Longman, Penguin España, Calle San Nicolas 15, E-28013 Madrid, Spain.*

In Japan: For a complete list of books available from Penguin in Japan, please write to *Longman Penguin Japan Co Ltd, Yamaguchi Building, 2-12-9 Kanda Jimbocho, Chiyoda-Ku, Tokyo 101, Japan.*

☐ **THE WOMEN OF BREWSTER PLACE**
  A Novel in Seven Stories
  Gloria Naylor

Winner of the American Book Award, this is the story of seven survivors of an urban housing project — a blind alley feeding into a dead end. From a variety of backgrounds, they experience, fight against, and sometimes transcend the fate of black women in America today.

192 pages   *ISBN: 0-14-006690-X*   **$5.95**

☐ **STONES FOR IBARRA**
  Harriet Doerr

An American couple comes to the small Mexican village of Ibarra to reopen a copper mine, learning much about life and death from the deeply faithful villagers.   *214 pages*   *ISBN: 0-14-007562-3*   **$5.95**

☐ **WORLD'S END**
  T. Coraghessan Boyle

"Boyle has emerged as one of the most inventive and verbally exuberant writers of his generation," writes *The New York Times*. Here he tells the story of Walter Van Brunt, who collides with early American history while searching for his lost father.   *456 pages*   *ISBN: 0-14-009760-0*   **$8.95**

☐ **THE WHISPER OF THE RIVER**
  Ferrol Sams

The story of Porter Osborn, Jr., who, in 1938, leaves his rural Georgia home to face the world at Willingham University, *The Whisper of the River* is peppered with memorable characters and resonates with the details of place and time. Ferrol Sams's writing is regional fiction at its best.

528 pages   *ISBN: 0-14-008387-1*   **$6.95**

☐ **ENGLISH CREEK**
  Ivan Doig

Drawing on the same heritage he celebrated in *This House of Sky*, Ivan Doig creates a rich and varied tapestry of northern Montana and of our country in the late 1930s.   *338 pages*   *ISBN: 0-14-008442-8*   **$6.95**

☐ **THE YEAR OF SILENCE**
  Madison Smartt Bell

A penetrating look at the varied reactions to a young woman's suicide exactly one year later, *The Year of Silence* "captures vividly and poignantly the chancy dance of life." (*The New York Times Book Review*)

208 pages   *ISBN: 0-14-011533-1*   **$6.95**

FOR THE BEST IN CONTEMPORARY AMERICAN FICTION

☐ **IN THE COUNTRY OF LAST THINGS**
Paul Auster

Death, joggers, leapers, and Object Hunters are just some of the realities of future city life in this spare, powerful, visionary novel about one woman's struggle to live and love in a frightening post-apocalyptic world.

208 pages   ISBN: 0-14-009705-8   **$5.95**

☐ **BETWEEN C&D**
New Writing from the Lower East Side Fiction Magazine
Joel Rose and Catherine Texier, Editors

A startling collection of stories by Tama Janowitz, Gary Indiana, Kathy Acker, Barry Yourgrau, and others, *Between C&D* is devoted to short fiction that ignores preconceptions — fiction not found in conventional literary magazines.

194 pages   ISBN: 0-14-010570-0   **$7.95**

☐ **LEAVING CHEYENNE**
Larry McMurtry

The story of a love triangle unlike any other, *Leaving Cheyenne* follows the three protagonists — Gideon, Johnny, and Molly — over a span of forty years, until all have finally "left Cheyenne."

254 pages   ISBN: 0-14-005221-6   **$6.95**

You can find all these books at your local bookstore, or use this handy coupon for ordering:

Penguin Books By Mail
Dept. BA Box 999
Bergenfield, NJ 07621-0999

Please send me the above title(s). I am enclosing _____
(please add sales tax if appropriate and $1.50 to cover postage and handling). Send check or money order—no CODs. Please allow four weeks for shipping. We cannot ship to post office boxes or addresses outside the USA. *Prices subject to change without notice.*

Ms./Mrs./Mr. _____

Address _____

City/State _____ Zip _____

Sales tax: CA: 6.5%   NY: 8.25%   NJ: 6%   PA: 6%   TN: 5.5%

FOR THE BEST LITERATURE, LOOK FOR THE

☐ **THE BOOK AND THE BROTHERHOOD**
Iris Murdoch

Many years ago Gerard Hernshaw and his friends banded together to finance a political and philosophical book by a monomaniacal Marxist genius. Now opinions have changed, and support for the book comes at the price of moral indignation; the resulting disagreements lead to passion, hatred, a duel, murder, and a suicide pact.　　　　　　　　　*602 pages*　*ISBN: 0-14-010470-4*　**$8.95**

☐ **GRAVITY'S RAINBOW**
Thomas Pynchon

Thomas Pynchon's classic antihero is Tyrone Slothrop, an American lieutenant in London whose body anticipates German rocket launchings. Surely one of the most important works of fiction produced in the twentieth century, *Gravity's Rainbow* is a complex and awesome novel in the great tradition of James Joyce's *Ulysses*.　　　　　　　　　*768 pages*　*ISBN: 0-14-010661-8*　**$10.95**

☐ **FIFTH BUSINESS**
Robertson Davies

The first novel in the celebrated "Deptford Trilogy," which also includes *The Manticore* and *World of Wonders*, *Fifth Business* stands alone as the story of a rational man who discovers that the marvelous is only another aspect of the real.　　　　　　　　　*266 pages*　*ISBN: 0-14-004387-X*　**$4.95**

☐ **WHITE NOISE**
Don DeLillo

Jack Gladney, a professor of Hitler Studies in Middle America, and his fourth wife, Babette, navigate the usual rocky passages of family life in the television age. Then, their lives are threatened by an "airborne toxic event"—a more urgent and menacing version of the "white noise" of transmissions that typically engulfs them.　　　　　　　　　*326 pages*　*ISBN: 0-14-007702-2*　**$7.95**
